The
Magic Half

The Magic Half

ANNIE BARROWS

BLOOMSBURY

NEW YORK BERLIN LONDON

Published by Bloomsbury U.S.A. Children's Books
175 Fifth Avenue, New York, New York 10010

The Library of Congress has cataloged the hardcover edition as follows:
Barrows, Annie.
The magic half / by Annie Barrows. — 1st U.S. ed.
p.   cm.
Summary: Eleven-year-old Miri Gill feels left out in her family, which has two sets of
twins and her, until she travels back in time to 1935 and discovers Molly, her own lost
twin, and brings her back to the present day.
ISBN-13: 978-1-59990-132-9 • ISBN-10: 1-59990-132-3 (hardcover)
[1. Twins—Fiction. 2. Time travel—Fiction. 3. Brothers and sisters—Fiction.] I. Title.
PZ7.B27576Mag 2008   [Fic]—dc22   2007023551

ISBN-13: 978-1-59990-358-3 • ISBN-10: 1-59990-358-X (paperback)

Typeset by Westchester Book Composition
Printed in the U.S.A. by Quebecor World Fairfield
1 3 5 7 9 10 8 6 4 2

For Jeffrey

The
Magic Half

⤳ CHAPTER ⤶

1

ONLY MIRI HAD NO TWIN. People always said, "Two sets of twins! That must have been quite a surprise!" They would smile at Miri's parents and shake their heads in wonder.

When she was younger, Miri had been proud of it. After all, as her father loved to remind them, only one in fifty thousand families had two pairs of twins. It was like being world champion of something. But after a while, Miri noticed that none of the smiling people ever looked at her. Their eyes moved from Ray and Robbie on one side to Nell and Nora on the other, slipping right over Miri in the middle.

"What about two pairs of twins and an extra?" Miri had asked once. She was curled up on the old blue couch in her father's cozy office. "How many families have that?"

Her father had turned a slow circle in his swivel chair before he answered. "I don't think they have statistics like that, baby. But you're part of a special family."

Ha, she thought, burrowing into the faded pillows. I'm just the extra, not the special.

Now the couch was gone, and she missed it. It had been sold, along with all the other things that Miri's mother had decided weren't good enough to move to the new house. It would probably be months before the new owner of the couch discovered that Miri had cut a hunk out of the bottom of one of the cushions to remember it by. Miri smiled craftily at herself in the bathroom mirror.

She had to admit that the new house wasn't all bad. The bathroom mirror was tinted pink, for instance, which made her look good. The bathroom door locked, too. Since they moved, Miri had spent a lot of time in there. "Hello, me," she said pleasantly to her pink reflection. She had toothpaste on her nose. She wiped it away, and a little breeze wafted a piece of hair over her forehead. The new house was full of breezes that seemed to come from nowhere. "We're going to freeze this winter," Miri told her reflection. Like an answer, another gust ruffled her hair.

Miri shook her half-straight, half-curly hair over her face. Her glasses glinted through the strands, so she took them off. *I'm the Wolf Princess,* she thought, *cursed to take on wolfish form when the moon grows full. My terrified family locks me in the bathroom, fearful of the destruction I may cause.* Miri paused to snarl wolfishly and then continued, *Shut up and forgotten, I spend years in solitude, eating bread that my family shoves under the door. But one night, as the full moon rises, I escape out the window*—Miri squinted at the bathroom window. She thought it looked big enough—*and tear through the countryside, causing mayhem among the villagers. Only one person is brave*—brave *enough to pursue the Wolf Princess*—*and his name is*—

"Miri!" her mother called down the hall. "Have you seen the girls?"

Miri put her glasses back on. "No."

There was a pause. "What are you doing in there?" asked her mother, outside the bathroom door now.

"Nothing." *Even in her human guise, the Wolf Princess had long, silvery hair that shone strangely in the moonlight.*

"Come down and have some breakfast, then."

Farewell, Wolf Princess, said Miri silently and opened the door. Her mother looked at her with a questioning smile. "You okay?"

"Don't you think I'd look cool with silver hair?"

Her mother considered. "At sixty, yes. At eleven, no."

The big, square kitchen, filled with summer light, was empty. But Nell and Nora had been there: an almost-empty ice-cream carton lay in a thickening mint-chip puddle on the counter. Miri's mom walked to the stove and poured herself a large cup of coffee. She contemplated the mess gloomily. "Those girls are a menace," she said.

Miri stood next to her. "It's not so bad," she said. "Remember the time they cut the eggs with scissors?"

Her mother giggled. "You're right. That was worse. I guess they're trying to tell me that they're tired of cereal." She opened a cupboard and scanned the shelves. "There's nothing else to eat, though. I should go to the store today. But what I really should be doing is setting up my office." She tapped her fingers against the cupboard door. "I wish your daddy wasn't at that stupid conference. I don't see why *anybody* needs to talk about geothermal energy for ten days, much less a man who— Oh my God!"

Miri looked up, startled. Her mother was gazing in horror at the back porch. Standing outside the screen door were Ray and Robbie. Their T-shirts were streaked with mud and dust. Their hair was thick with cobwebs, and their faces, underneath smears of grime, were blazing with enthusiasm. "Hey!" Ray yelled. "You'll never guess what!"

"What happened to you? What are you doing out there? Don't come inside!"

"Guess what, Mom!" Ray bellowed. "There's stolen stuff! In the house!"

Robbie nodded, beaming.

"Excuse me?" said Miri's mom.

"We met a guy! Who told us!" Ray hollered, as if they were miles away instead of just on the other side of the screen.

"*Stop!*" ordered their mother. She looked sternly at her sons. "Ray, please stop yelling. Robbie, can you tell me—quietly—why you're filthy and what stolen stuff you're talking about? And who this guy is?" She nodded at Robbie. "Begin."

Miri's mother was on a campaign to get Robbie to talk more.

Robbie was having none of it. He jerked his head at Ray. "Let him tell."

Ray smirked at his mother and continued, "As I was saying, we got up superearly this morning, like so early the sun was rising, cause we're going to do track when school starts, and we thought we should start training today. So we decided to run to the creek, swim around in the swimming hole, and run back." He slapped himself proudly on the stomach. "Cross-training."

"And then?" prompted his mother.

"And then," Ray continued, "we ran through the woods. We did great. Except Robbie tripped on a root or something and cut himself because he's a dweeb." Robbie smacked his brother on the back of the head. "Get out," said Ray, smacking him in return. "Anyway, we were trying to run without any sound, like those Indian dudes, but Robbie made a lot of noise when he fell and Mr. Guest heard us."

Miri imagined running from tree to tree, silent as

air. Maybe sometime she could go along with them. "Who's Mr. Guest?" she asked.

"He's the guy!" Ray said impatiently.

Which guy? wondered Miri.

But Ray was continuing, "He said we scared all the fish away when we were running around in the woods, even though we didn't really make that much noise. Anyway, he's this old guy, like really old, who's lived in the valley for a million years, and you know what he says? He says—"

"He says there's stolen stuff under our house!" Robbie blurted.

"Under this house?" said Mom doubtfully.

"Well, it might be under the house," Ray said. "Mr. Guest said 'on the property.' But no one knows where. He says way back in the twenties or something there was a guy who lived here who was a thief, and he buried the junk he stole here, and after he was gone, nobody ever found it. It could be jewelry, he said. Isn't that *sick?*"

His mother smiled at him. "That's pretty sick, all right."

"Maybe it's bones," said Robbie in a dreamy voice.

"It better not be," said Mom firmly. "So—let me guess how you got all those cobwebs in your hair. You crawled under the house to look for this stuff. Right?"

"Yeah. So far, though, we only found a rake," said Ray. "We're going to look some more after breakfast. We're starving," he added.

Robbie nodded vigorously.

"I'll get you all some cereal," said Mom. "But boys, I'm not so crazy about the idea of you messing around under the house. There's a lot of nasty stuff under houses, and your father will have a fit if you knock out any of those furnace ducts. Why don't you look in the yard?"

"Mom!" groaned Ray. "A thief wouldn't put his loot out in the yard where anyone could find it. That'd be stupid! He'd have buried it under the house, in a hidden place." Robbie nodded in agreement.

"You know," said Mom hopefully, "there was a barn on this property a long time ago. It was some-where out in back, near the apple trees, I think. He could have buried it in the barn."

"Mom! Come on! We're not complete morons. We won't touch the furnace, we promise. Just let us look under the house. Please!"

Their mother sighed. "All of my children are horribly stubborn." She yanked gently on Miri's hair. "All except you, thank goodness. Okay, boys, you can look under the house, but carefully. Don't touch the furnace or the water heater. And watch out for spiders."

"Can I help?" asked Miri eagerly.

Ray and Robbie glanced at each other. Then Robbie gave her one of his wide, sweet smiles and said, "Maybe later you can help, Miri. Today, Ray and I want it to be just us. Okay?" Saying no to Miri was always his job.

"Now guys, that's not right," objected Mom. "If there's buried loot, it's as much Miri's as yours. But honey," she turned to Miri, her face pleading, "it's your turn to look after the girls this morning. The boys will do it this afternoon—oh, don't give me that look, you two—and Miri, you can go look for buried treasure then. But this morning, I have to get my office unpacked. My syllabus is due next Tuesday, and I can't even *find* most of my files."

Miri nodded, but she said nothing. That wasn't what she wanted—to go hunting alone. She wanted to crawl under the house with Ray and Robbie. She wanted to dig in the mysterious dirt. She wanted to hear her shovel knock against a hard surface and call out, Hey, guys, I think I hit something. She wanted them to come rushing over to her spot and scrape frantically, all three of them, until the dull shine of a metal box appeared in the flashlight beam. She wanted them to let out an admiring breath and say, Wow, Miri, you did it. But that's not what they wanted. They just wanted each other.

Her mother slipped an arm around her shoulder. "You know how much I appreciate it, honey. Tell you what. Next week, after my deadline, we'll go hunting together. We'll find that old treasure before the boys do."

∿ CHAPTER ∿

2

"STOP YELLING about that stupid doll!" It was Ray's voice.

"Sierra is my baby and I'm the mommy!" Nell was screeching.

"She's *not* Sierra, she's Amber!" hollered Nora.

"Who *cares* about your ugly doll?" thundered Robbie.

Out in the leafy backyard, Miri turned in time to see a naked doll sail out the back door and land with a thud in a pile of dust. Instantly, shrill screams erupted from Nell and Nora, together with aggravated yells from Robbie and Ray. Miri giggled. Her brothers were finally babysitting their little sisters, and she was glad to see that they were being driven out of their minds. Served them right. Robbie and Ray had a genius for disappearing when they were supposed to watch Nell and Nora.

Feeling free, Miri turned and wandered down the faint dirt path that led through the lawn to an enormous overgrown tangle of blackberry bushes. The new house was much larger than their tidy home in the city, but it was more disorganized, too, with rooms popping out on the sides and a saggy porch in the back. Its gray paint was peeling, but the roof was edged with lacy carved wood, heavy vines cloaked the front porch in green shadows, and there were stained glass windows that sent jeweled light shimmering through the hallway at sunset. Her mother called it "decayed grandeur," but Miri thought it was old-fashioned beautiful.

The garden was the same way—big, old, and shabby. When Miri first saw it, she had supposed that the circular lawn, with its shady elm and white gazebo, was the whole backyard.

"Nope," her father had said. "The nice part stops at the lawn, but it's all ours, past those ugly bushes and back through the woods to the creek. Used to be a farm, I guess. I think that overgrown part next to the driveway was an apple orchard."

Now Miri picked her way through the stickery berry coils, looking for a sign of the barn that her mother had mentioned that morning. Stopping in the humming sunshine, she popped a blackberry into her mouth and it exploded in hot, sweet juice. If she lived in the woods, she would live on berries, nuts, and roots, which she would collect in a little basket she'd weave herself from reeds. Miri picked up a few walnut shells that lay in the dust at her feet. They would be her little cups. She would fill them with berry juice and flower nectar. Then, on the night of the full moon, she'd be awakened by dozens of tiny blue fairies with swishing silver wings. Each would take a dainty sip of the drink and pat their mouths with their gossamer hankies. In a thin, silvery voice, the Queen Fairy would call out, "You, Miriam, have given us hospitality, and in return we will make you one of us this night." Together with the fairies, Miri would flutter through the dark woods, talking to the night birds.

"Whatsamatter, Miri? You get stung by a bee?" yelled Ray from the back porch. Miri turned to find four pairs of eyes gazing at her as she fluttered back and forth across the grass, inside her fairy world.

"Stop watching me, you guys! Leave me alone!"

Miri ran around the blackberry bushes to find a secluded spot where she could pretend in peace.

But even in the shade of the dusty bushes, Miri was embarrassed. Fairies. At her age. Last year her teacher, Mrs. Lorne, had written on her report card, "Miri has a dazzling imaginative capacity." That sounded nice, but most of the other fifth-grade girls had stopped pretending. They would act out movies or maybe books, but they thought magic was for babies. Mostly, they just walked together, talking and giggling. Except for Lili. Lili would pretend anything Miri wanted. She had even changed her name from Lillian to Lili to be more like Miri. The only problem with Lili was she didn't do any of the pretending herself. She just waited for Miri to tell her what to do. Still, Miri admitted to herself, it would feel good to see Lili right this minute.

Miri sighed. Her glasses slipped down her sweaty nose, and she pushed them up to look out at the empty expanse of grass and weeds that stretched before her to the woods. Of course, it wasn't really empty. There were clumps of rocks and bushes, even a few stray stacks of wood. Miri got to her feet, planning to cross through the weeds and head for the stream that wandered through the trees behind. She climbed across a row of rocks and a few mounds of dirt to reach the cool shade of the trees. Then she stopped.

Wait.

A row of rocks. Why would rocks be in a row? She turned to investigate. The rocks were not really rocks, but lumps of gray brick in a broken line. Miri peered around at the surrounding area. Yes—over there was a pile of collapsed wood. And there was another straight line of bricks. Out from under the blowzy blackberry bush, another stack of rotting boards jutted forward, and an old metal wheel leaned against an uneven bit of fence. An ancient bucket filled with hard, dry dirt sat next to a scrubby bush. This was it, she thought excitedly—the barn! Now she could see its outline. It was definitely the ruins of an old building, and the only old building it could be was the barn her mother had mentioned that morning. Miri found a sturdy branch, and, starting from the broken gray bricks, she drew a long line out to the pile of collapsed boards. There was one wall. Carefully, she traced three more walls by walking from fragment to fragment. There, she thought, looking at her work with satisfaction, that's the barn. The hidden barn. A hidden barn would be a perfect place to bury stolen jewels. I bet this is the place. The blackberry coils rustled in a sudden breath of air, cooling the sweat on her face. Miri nodded. This is definitely the place. I bet I could dig it up before the boys! I'll beat them to it. She pictured a little treasure chest glittering with coins and jewels. Rings were her favorites. Opal rings. She turned and raced back to the house to find a shovel.

Miri bounced through the screen door and began scrabbling through the boxes that littered the back porch. She found her mother's gardening gloves, and the shovel was probably nearby—

"Whatcha doing, Miri?" It was Ray, standing in the kitchen doorway. Miri jumped—she had forgotten about her brothers and sisters.

"Nothing," she answered. It was a dumb thing to say. Anybody could see that she was doing *something*. But she wanted to keep her discovery a secret. She wanted to find the treasure on her own and bring it back to show them. She had a vision of her brothers, exchanging impressed looks while she unclasped an ancient wooden chest. She would be modest about it. And kind. But she wasn't going to tell them what she was doing yet. They would only laugh. And why shouldn't I have a secret? she thought. Ray and Robbie won't let me hunt with them, so why should I tell them about my barn?

Ray didn't ask again. He just stood there and watched her, slitty-eyed. After a minute, Miri turned back to the pile of gardening stuff. There it was, the green shovel. Just exactly what she needed. Ray was still staring at her, she knew. She tried to think of something she could be doing with a shovel that wouldn't interest a twelve-year-old boy—digging for worms? No, he'd love that. Planting flowers? No, he'd know she didn't have seeds. Oh, it was too hard! Eager to find her treasure, Miri decided to make a run for it.

She tried an old trick. "Oh no!" she exclaimed, looking over Ray's shoulder with a horrified expression.

"What?" he said quickly, turning around.

As fast as a cat, Miri hurled herself out the screen door, jumped over the stairs, and raced madly across the grass.

She should have known it wouldn't work. After

all, Ray and Robbie were going to be track stars next year. With a whoop, Ray leaped out the back door and chased her. Robbie, who had no idea what it was all about, joined in because he was bored and it looked like fun. Ray grabbed Miri's arm and began to pull on it, but she kicked him and broke away. "Go away! Leave me alone!" she yelled and ran wildly toward the blackberry bushes.

"Get her!" Ray croaked to Robbie, who stuck out one leg and tripped her.

Miri went sprawling, and as she did, she heard the distinctive crunch of her glasses cracking. "Oh no! You broke my glasses!" she shouted, picking herself up from the grass. "You broke my glasses, you big creeps!" Tears of rage sprang into her eyes, and she tried again to run from her tormentors.

But they didn't stop. To them, it was a game. And if it was a game, they had to win it. "Head her off!" yowled Ray. He made a headfirst dive and succeeded in grabbing her around the stomach. Robbie cheered him on.

"You jerk! I hate you!" screamed Miri. She pulled her arm free, and, in an explosion of fury, brought her shovel down with a clunk on Ray's head. There was a short silence, and he dropped to the ground. Instantly, shrill squeals burst from the back porch, where Nell and Nora had been a happy audience to the brawl, and Robbie jumped to his feet and ran to his brother's side.

"Mom! Mom!" he yelled, catching hold of Ray's shirt and trying to drag him toward the house. "C'mere! Miri killed Ray!"

A new wave of screams poured from the porch, and Miri, sobbing now with fear, saw her mother moving in a blur of speed from the back door toward Ray.

"Raymond!" her mother said in a low, urgent voice.

"Mmm," he replied in a whisper. "I'm okay I think."

"Don't sit up yet," she said, patting him. "Where does it hurt?"

"My *head*," he said, wincing.

"Miri clocked him with the shovel, Mom! I couldn't believe it! She just slammed him right on the head—" Robbie babbled.

Her mother turned toward Miri, her face terrible. "Did you hit your brother with a shovel?"

Miri tried to explain, "They were grabbing me, Mom! They broke my glasses, and they wouldn't leave me alone, and they followed me, and then Ray knocked me over and—"

"Miriam Gill, did you hit your brother on the head with a shovel?" Her mother's voice was tight and furious.

"Yes," said Miri, looking at the grass. "But he—"

"You could have killed him, Miri! How would you have felt then?" Her mother's face was white. Miri had never seen her so angry. "Hitting is absolutely not acceptable in this family!" Miri tried again to explain, but her mother interrupted. "I don't want to hear a word! Not a word! Get up to your room this minute! This *minute!*" She spit the word.

"But—"

"Your room!" Her mother pointed a jabbing finger toward the house.

There was a silence, and Miri felt the stares of Ray and Robbie, Nell and Nora against her skin. She stuffed her broken glasses into the pocket of her dress and walked stiffly across the grass. When she opened the back door, Nell and Nora drew in their breath, as though they were shocked to find themselves in the company of such a bad person. Miri turned around and looked at Ray, who was sitting up on the grass with Robbie at his side. A mocking grin flickered across his face, and he stuck his tongue out at her. "He's just faking it!" Miri yelled.

Ray resumed his pathetic expression just as his mother swirled around. "Your *room!*" she shouted to Miri with another jab of her finger.

∻ CHAPTER ∻

3

INSIDE, THE HOUSE was shadowy and quiet. Miri brushed her fingertips along the smooth, dark wood of the hallway and felt a little comforted. Her face was hot with anger and running, and her eyes were swollen from tears; she wished she could find a little door in the wall and disappear. Slowly, she climbed the small staircase that led to her room. Her room. She stopped on the threshold and peered at the walls. It didn't look any better without glasses.

When her parents decided to move from their house in Stanton far away into the valley, they had made a big deal about Miri finally getting her own room, instead of sharing with Nell and Nora. And, though Miri had been worried about leaving her friends and the house she had lived in all her life, she thought that having her own room would make up for a lot.

It didn't. Separated from the rest of the upper story by a steep, narrow staircase that was more like a ladder, her room had clearly been part of the attic at one time. Rather than being a rectangle or a square, the walls—and there were a lot of them—formed a peculiar shape. "It's not exactly an octagon, is it?" said her mother doubtfully, as they stood looking at the room for the first time.

Her father counted silently. "It's a decagon," he announced after a moment. "Ten sides. That's pretty cool."

There were two thin windows on one side of the room, and then one more, a tiny, round, porthole-like window set high on the east side.

"It's like a skylight that slid," said Ray.

It wasn't exactly what Miri had been imagining, but she could have been excited about the strange shape and the weird windows if it hadn't been for the wallpaper. "Now don't worry about the wall-paper," her mother said brightly. "We'll get that taken care of in no time!" No time wasn't soon enough. The wallpaper was dark purple striped with vines of orange leaves. It was the ugliest wallpaper Miri had ever seen. And the closet was strange, too. It was almost as big as the room itself and had a long, low seat built into one wall.

"Who'd want to sit down inside a closet?" muttered Miri, sitting down.

Robbie pushed his way into the closet and leaned close to her ear. "It's a coffin," he whispered in a ghostly voice. "Prepare to die."

"Get out of here," said Miri, giggling.

But at night when she lay in bed, she wondered.

. . .

Now, as Miri stood in the doorway, the small room felt like a jail cell. Or maybe an oven. It was sweltering. She thought of Ray's flickering smile and slammed the door behind her. What a liar he was! "Too bad I didn't hurt him for real," she mumbled, stomping toward her old rocking chair, "as long as I'm in trouble anyway." She thumped down in her chair and began rocking wildly back and forth while she tried to guess what her punishment would be. It would be something pretty bad, she knew, because her mother hated it when they hit each other. Probably she'd be grounded. Big deal. There was no place to go anyway. Her mom would likely realize this. Maybe she'd have to go to bed early for a week. Or a month. Or maybe she'd have to stay in her room all day. She'd broil. She'd suffocate, and then they'd all feel really bad. Sweat trickled down Miri's neck, and she looked around at the purple walls in disgust. They were all liars, everyone in her family. Wasn't the wallpaper supposed to be gone by now? "We'll paint it any color you like, sweetie," her mother had said. But it had been twelve days, and she was still stuck with the grossest wallpaper in the world. Without her glasses, she couldn't see the orange vines clearly, but there was a sort of a stripy orange tinge to the walls. Orange and purple wallpaper—who would be crazy enough to choose orange and purple wallpaper? Some old lady. Her mother had said that the house had belonged to an old, old lady who had lived there a long time. I bet she just picked this wallpaper on purpose to make the room uglier, thought Miri. I bet she put the wallpaper up right before she moved out, just to be mean. She knew this wasn't true—the wallpaper was old and faded—but it made her feel better.

Suddenly, Miri stopped rocking. There, in one of the many corners of the room, something glinted. Miri screwed up her eyes. It flashed like glass or a mirror. Her heart began to thump as she rose from her chair and walked toward the small, shining spot. Maybe, she thought, it's a tiny window.

But it wasn't. It was just a piece of glass, taped to the wooden board that separated the wall from the floor. Miri knelt down to get a better look, her dark hair tumbling forward. It was shaped like the glass in a pair of eyeglasses. It was a single lens from a pair of glasses—just the lens—stuck to the paint with a strip of yellowing tape. Carefully, Miri pulled the tape back, and the thin oval of glass fell into her hand. As it touched her skin, one of the stray breezes that wafted through the house grazed her, and a shiver rippled down Miri's backbone. The surface of the lens was gray with dust. Why would anyone stick a piece of glass onto a wall? she wondered. She blew some of the dust away and then wiped the lens on her dress. There. Now it was clear enough to see through. She winked one eye closed and lifted the glass to the other.

Her eye filled with tears, and the purple walls around her wavered and bubbled. Wow. Whoever owned these glasses had really terrible eyesight, thought Miri. She rubbed the tears from her eye and then held up the glass again. This time the room seemed to bend and collapse in the middle, as though the center of the house were being sucked into a whirlpool, but Miri hardly noticed, because her attention had been caught by something else, something very strange indeed. She could suddenly hear voices. They sounded very close, as though they came from the landing at the bottom of the stairs. And they were not voices that Miri had ever heard before.

"And I'd better not catch you again." A young woman's voice was raised in irritation. "Or you're going to owe me a brand-new lipstick!"

A door opened in the hall. "What'd she do now?" a voice growled. It was a teenage boy's voice, but low and thick, and Miri felt her heart begin to race. What was happening?

"She's been messing with my lipstick—again. Ma! Molly's fooling with my bureau again!" the young woman called out.

"Want me to get her?" the boy asked. He laughed, but his laugh didn't sound very funny. "I'll get her for you." A heavy footstep sounded on the stair.

Miri looked wildly around the room. There was

something about the boy's voice—especially his laugh—that gave her the creeps. Even if this was completely crazy and she was having sunstroke, she knew for sure that she didn't want the owner of that voice to find her.

The heavy steps came closer, and Miri made a leap into the closet. The long space was filled with unfamiliar items: thick coats and suitcases and boxes that Miri had never laid eyes on before. She didn't have a moment to do more than wonder at this mystery before she squeezed between a heavy woolen coat and a pointy cardboard box. The bedroom door was shoved open and Miri held her breath.

From somewhere far below came the thin, silvery ringing of a bell.

The boy let out a surprised-sounding grunt, "Hnnh?" Then Miri heard him thundering down the stairs. The young woman, too, seemed to be running away, or at least Miri could hear the clattering of heels on the wooden floor growing fainter and fainter.

Then there was silence. Miri waited.

Long minutes slid by.

Nothing happened.

Finally, with cautious steps, Miri eased out of her hiding place. Slowly, quietly, she tiptoed to the closet door and peeked into her bedroom. Except that it wasn't her bedroom anymore. The walls still stood, all ten of them, and so did the funny long windows and even the little porthole, but everything else was different. The hateful wallpaper was gone, and in its place was a faded pattern of pink roses on white. The stack of cardboard boxes containing Miri's books no longer towered in one corner; a scratched dressing table filled the space instead. And where Miri's bright blue bed had been a few minutes before, a small white bed with a faded pink bedspread stood. There was a limp rag rug on the floor, and at its center rested a battered old doll carriage containing a sleeping white cat. The doll itself, bald and chewed-looking, poked its head out from under the bed.

Miri looked slowly around the room, observing each new item in order to hold off the panic rising within her. What had happened? Where had her room gone? "Have I gone nuts?" she murmured, and the sound of her own voice in this strange place frightened her even more. She looked at the cat, whose unconcerned sleep was slightly comforting, and tried to remember if she had ever seen him before. Could she have walked into a different room by mistake? After all, they had only lived in the house for twelve days—maybe she had taken a wrong turn. But that was completely ridiculous; the house wasn't so big that it could have rooms she'd never seen before, especially not rooms with ten walls. Yes, the walls were the same, and the windows. It *was* her room, but—somehow—completely changed.

Like a sleepwalker, she went to a window and looked out, hoping to see her mother, brothers, and sisters on the great lawn below. She wouldn't mind being yelled at, she wouldn't even mind being chased and knocked down. She just wanted a familiar face. She took one look and drew her breath in sharply. Even without her glasses, she could tell that there was no sign of her mother on the lawn below, nor of her brothers, nor of her sisters. What's more, the backyard was different, too. The elm tree was shorter and thinner and much less shady, but what made Miri gasp was the barn. There it was, a weathered gray barn with something that looked like a pigpen on one side, and it was standing in exactly the position Miri had so recently discovered behind the blackberry bushes. The bushes themselves were gone now, and when Miri squinted, she saw neat rows of vegetables in their place.

The sound of a screen door crashing into its frame shook Miri from her daze. Quickly, she pulled back from the window. If it wasn't her house, it was somebody else's, and maybe that somebody wouldn't be pleased to find her here.

No sooner had this thought occurred to Miri than the door opened soundlessly and a girl about her own age slipped quickly inside. She closed the door behind her and made a flying leap into the closet. There was a moment of complete silence, during which Miri wondered what on earth she should do, and then a pair of large gray eyes peeked around the edge of the closet door.

"Oh my gosh!" the girl said in a whisper. "You're here."

∴ CHAPTER ∾

4

MIRI'S MOUTH OPENED, but no words came out. What could she say? The girl was apparently expecting her, which made *Who are you?* sound very rude.

The girl didn't seem to mind. She was busy staring at Miri. A long minute passed, and then she blurted, "Will you show me your wand? Please?"

"Excuse me?" said Miri.

"Your *wand*," the girl repeated.

"Um. I don't have a wand," said Miri slowly. She wished she did. The girl's thick-lashed eyes were glowing with admiration and excitement, and Miri didn't want to disappoint her. "I'm Miri Gill," she said, to change the subject. "What's your name?"

"Oh!" The girl looked embarrassed. "Molly. Molly Gardner. I thought you knew."

Miri felt as though she had fallen into the middle of a play where everyone knew their lines except her. "Why?" she burst out. "How could I know your name when I never saw you before in my whole life?"

The girl grinned at her, a can't-fool-me grin. "You're trying to test me. Fairies do that all the time. Grandma May and me called you up, and you're a fairy, so of course you know my name."

Miri began to feel dizzy. "I'm *not* a fairy, and nobody called me up. I was just sitting in my room—this room—and then it all switched, and I was here, and I don't understand any of this . . ." She trailed off.

"You are too a fairy," Molly said firmly. "Otherwise what are you doing in my room?"

"I don't *know* what I'm doing in your room. And it's my room, by the way—at least it was a few minutes ago. It had purple wallpaper."

Molly glanced quickly around at the faded pink wallpaper and the old iron bed. "It did not," she retorted. "It's been like this since my mama was a girl, 'cause it used to be her room."

"But it's my room," said Miri weakly. "Is this 2207 Pickering Lane?"

Now Molly goggled at her. "It's Pickering Lane, all right, but it's not twenty-two-whatever-you-said. It's just the country out here—there's only three houses on the whole road. We don't need numbers to tell one from the other."

Just the country. Only three houses on the lane. A strange notion began to take shape in Miri's mind. It was impossible, and yet—it happened in books. She shook her head; it was a crazy idea. But there was the barn in the backyard, and the elm, smaller and less leafy. Just the country. She held herself still and listened intently, and in the hot air she heard only the buzz of cicadas and the distracted cackle of afternoon birds. No cars. Let's look at this logically, she thought, trying to hold back the tide of excitement that flooded her. It's definitely the same room. But maybe—just maybe—it's not the same time. "What year is it?" she asked urgently.

Molly smiled at her triumphantly. "You see? You are too a fairy. You don't even know what year it is because you're from the shadowed ages of the past."

"Fine. I'm a fairy. What year is it?"

"1935."

"1935!" Miri sat down abruptly on the limp rag rug. This was crazy. This was completely unexplainable. Things like this don't happen, she thought. She lifted her head to look once again around the half-familiar room and took a gaspy breath. In books, people who traveled through time always knew immediately what they had done. None of them got sick to their stomachs either.

She felt a small, sweaty hand patting her on the back.

It was Molly. She crouched beside Miri, her brown braids tickling Miri's shoulder. "Don't fret," she whispered. "I won't let 'em catch you, if that's what you're fussing about. Most people don't even believe in you anymore, so it's a lot safer than it used to be."

"That's good," said Miri. "I guess."

Molly nodded encouragingly. "Everything will be all right. You'll do just fine."

Miri stared at her. "What will I do just fine?" she asked. "What am I going to do?"

"Why," said Molly, nodding, "you know. Grandma May summoned you up to save me, or"—Molly blushed—"I sort of summoned you for her, since she doesn't talk anymore. She talks to me with her eyes, and she told me what to do. I thought I hadn't done it right, 'cause nothing happened for a while, but I guess I did okay." She smiled broadly. "I guess I did better than okay."

Miri looked at Molly's thin, eager face. Her gray eyes were shining under the thick black lashes, and when she spoke her hands waved, as if they wanted to speak as well. Even her dark braids seemed to leap along with her words. "What am I supposed to be saving you from?" Miri asked.

"Horst," said Molly simply, and a shadow covered the light in her face for a moment. "Horst for sure. And Aunt Florence. And Sissy, too, but she's not as bad as the other two. Mostly Horst and Aunt Flo. You're supposed to get me out of here and take me to a nice family. A nice family who will take care of me." She smiled in anticipation and her face was once again alight.

"Is Horst that boy I heard?" Miri guessed. He had sounded like someone you'd want to be saved from.

"Yeah. He's my cousin," said Molly. The clouded

look returned as she thought of him. "Him and Sissy both are."

"You don't have a mom or dad?" Miri asked slowly.

"No mama," Molly said, her eyes fixed on the faded wall before her. "I have a dad, but he's away on business."

"Oh," said Miri.

"He's been away on business for about six years," added Molly.

No mom, no dad, a sick grandma, and a bunch of mean cousins. Even with rotten creep brothers and no twin, Miri's family was better than that. She felt sorry for what she was about to say. "Molly, I'm not a fairy. At least I don't think I am and I never was before and I don't have a clue about how to help you. I was just sitting in my room, which is this room about—um—seventy-five years from now. I know that sounds totally crazy, but it's true!" Molly was looking at her intently, but she didn't say anything. "I got sent to my room because I hit my brother with a shovel, but that's a different story—anyway, I was just sitting in my room, when all of a sudden I found this little piece of glass from a pair of eyeglasses, and then I looked through it and—" Miri opened her fist to show Molly the aged glass. It looked more fragile than ever. "And when I looked through it, everything changed." She stopped, staring at the little lens. "Everything wavered and kind of shivered . . ." Her voice trailed off. How could she describe it?

"And you came here," finished Molly, looking reverently at the slender piece of glass. "Seventy-five years. You're from the twenty-first century! Do people ride around in rockets?"

Miri shook her head. "Sometimes. Not very often."

But Molly wasn't listening. "You went back in time," she continued. "It's strange to think of now as back in time, but I'll get used to it. The thing of it is—it's magic!" Her eyes glowed. "Magic happened, to me! And you too, of course."

"Magic," said Miri, struck by the wonder of it. Could it be true? She looked at the ten walls of Molly's room, her room. A little wave of cool air broke into the throbbing afternoon heat, and Miri felt herself understand. Of course there was magic. Nothing else could explain her presence in this strange, familiar room. After all those years of wishing for magic, it had finally happened. To me, she thought to herself. It happened to me. An earthquake of joy shook her. "Oh boy," she whispered. Magic is real, her mind sang, magic is real—and it happened to *me*. "My heart is jumping all over the place," she said to Molly.

Molly's solemn face suddenly burst into a starry smile. "Me too," she confessed. "I've been hoping for this my whole life."

The two girls grinned at each other. There was such a thing as magic. Other people had laughed at them, but they had been right all along.

All at once, a rough roar exploded from the bottom of the stairs. "You up there, runt?" Molly jumped and put her finger to her lips. Miri nodded. It was the teenage boy again, and he was angrier than ever. "Thought you'd fool us, din't you?" he called out in a voice that sounded mean and glad at the same time. "Thought you'd ring Gran's bell and watch us jump, din't you?" The stairs creaked, and the boy huffed as he climbed them. "You're gonna be sorry when I find you."

Soundlessly, Molly reached over and grabbed

Miri by the collar of her dress, and with one sweeping yank pulled her into the long closet. Miri wondered desperately where they could hide—the boy didn't sound like someone who could be stopped by a few coats—but then, to her surprise, she saw Molly pull up the top of the long, low bench like a lid. "Get in," she whispered, gesturing frantically. "Get in and roll back."

Obediently, Miri climbed inside the bench and lay down, her back pressing against the wall. As the door of Molly's room was thrust open, Molly leaped into the narrow bench next to—or, really, on top of—Miri. "Push against the wall," she hissed, closing the lid over them.

What good is that? thought Miri, but the sharp yowl of the cat in the next room warned her not to argue. She pushed—and the wall opened like a door. It was hinged at the top inside the bench, like a cat door, and Miri rolled through it, out onto the dusty floor of an attic, praying that she had not been heard. An instant later, Molly was beside her, breathing heavily. She laid an unnecessary hand over Miri's mouth, and together they lay on the floor, listening to the furious muttering in the next room. "Someday,

Molly, someday I'm gonna make you sorry—see if I don't!" There was a pause filled with the sound of the doll carriage being knocked over. "Dang kid! I know she's somewhere around here laughing and thinking she's real cute." Now the boy stomped into the closet and shoved the heavy coats and dresses back and forth. Only a few inches away, in the attic, Miri tried with all her might to be motionless. Think frozen, she told herself. Think dead—no, that's what we'll be if he finds us. Don't think dead. Think frozen. Ice. Glaciers. The muttering went on and on, as though the boy had forgotten that he was talking. "Don't lift a finger. Does whatever she has a mind to. Who does the work around here? Not her, that's for sure. Ma and Sis and me, that's who, while she sucks up to Gran." There was a snort, as if the word *Gran* was particularly infuriating. "Who's been taking care of the crazy old bat all these years? Ma and Sis and me, that's who. But now we're just mud under her feet. Mud!" There was a thump as the boy pounded his fist against a sturdy portion of wall and then a yelp of surprise at the pain he had caused himself. Miri, glancing toward Molly, saw a smile cross her face.

"Runt!" the boy mumbled. "Runt!" Despite his

threats, he seemed to have given up on the project of finding Molly, for his voice faded and was replaced by the sound of heavy boots clumping down the narrow stairs. Lying side by side, the two girls let out a breath of relief.

"Was that Horst?" whispered Miri.

Molly nodded.

"He sounds awful."

"You ought to see him," said Molly darkly. "He looks worse than he sounds."

"What would he have done if he'd caught you?" asked Miri, worried.

Molly thought. "Mostly he just takes me to his ma and she whups me with her silver hairbrush, but I don't know—he's getting meaner. I make sure he doesn't catch me."

Miri looked toward the hinged door that led into the bench in the closet. "What if he finds out about that?"

Molly was unconcerned. "Oh, he won't. The one good thing about Horst is he's not so smart. He doesn't even know that the seat part lifts."

Miri wasn't going to admit that she hadn't known it herself. "I wonder who thought of making a door inside," she said.

"I did," said Molly simply.

Miri was impressed. This was a girl who got things done. "How'd you know how?"

Molly shrugged. "I didn't know how. But I needed a getaway, so I just borrowed Horst's saw and some hinges and stuff. It wasn't hard."

Miri looked around the dusty attic. Light slanted in through a faraway vent, and she could see a few boxes flung into corners. There was a wire dress-maker's dummy lying on the floor. She looked like she was taking a nap. Miri asked, "Why is he so mean to you?"

"He hates me," Molly said calmly, as if it were a regular thing to be hated.

"But why?"

"We can get up now," said Molly, raising herself and brushing off her wrinkled dress. "They all hate me. It's because Grandma May loved my mama and she loves me. Mama had the gift, see, and Aunt Flo never did, so of course she's jealous. And I've got it, too, probably."

Miri was tired of being confused. She sat up and said, "Okay, what's the gift?"

Molly looked at her suspiciously. "The *gift*," she said, as though Miri were hard of hearing. "I think you're just pretending not to know. The gift of *magic*. Grandma's part fairy, and so was my mama. And so am I. Probably. That's how come we could call you up."

Miri teetered on the brink of belief. After all, if she could get sucked through an eyeglass lens to 1935, there was no reason why Molly couldn't be a fairy. A little thrill shivered through her—there was no reason why she couldn't be a fairy herself! Maybe that's why she had never stopped pretending! Just for a second, she allowed herself to feel wings—silvery wings—on her back, but a furtive poke revealed only the usual bones and skin. If she were a fairy, she admitted, she probably would have noticed it before now. And, fairy or not, she had some questions. "Okay. The gift is magic. Okay. Got that. Why does that make Horst hate you?"

"Because," explained Molly, trying to be patient, "Horst—and Aunt Flo and Sissy—think that Grandma's going to give her money to me when she dies. Everybody says she's got secret riches, and they're all in a sweat that she's gonna tell me where they are. But she's never said anything to me about riches. And now she's awful sick." The shadows crossed her face again. "Seems like she's just fading away. But now it doesn't matter if they all hate me, because I'm going back with you. Right?" She smiled happily at Miri.

"Back where?" asked Miri, confused again.

"Back. To your time. Where you came from. I'm ready."

Miri stared at her. "You want to come home with me? But—but—what are you going to do when you get there? My mom'll freak out if I suddenly appear with you and say Hi Mom, here's another kid for you. Trust me, she'll freak." Miri spoke rapidly, trying to ignore the misery dropping over Molly's face. "And besides, you don't know what it's like in my time. You've got to have papers and things, and they'll stick you in some foster home, and they're mostly awful, at least I think they are—" She stopped.

Molly's gray eyes were swimming with tears, and her fingers were twisting up the fabric of her dress. The dress was too small, Miri saw, and there was a rip in the shoulder and on the worn skirt. Miri saw, too, that Molly's braids were crooked, the way braids always are if you try to do them by yourself. Molly didn't have anyone to take care of her, to fix her braids or get her a bigger dress. The thought pushed on Miri's throat. She looked at the slanting light on the attic wall. I'm no fairy, she thought glumly. I'm more like a goblin. What good is it for magic to be real if you don't let it happen? No, she suddenly decided, even if it is crazy, even if Mom has a total conniption fit, even if I get into a truly humongous amount of trouble, even if the whole thing's impossible anyway—I won't leave Molly behind.

"Okay," she said.

Molly looked up. "Okay what?"

"Okay, let's go back. So my mom will freak. So what? She's freaked before and she'll freak again." Miri tried to ignore the part of her brain that said, *Are you out of your mind? Your mom freaks about stuff like burping at the table, stuff that's not even close to this!*

"Miri," said Molly, holding up her hand as though she were making a pledge. "You're not going to regret it, I promise you. This is all the magic I need. You just get me there, and I'll do the rest. I promise I won't bother your mama, or anybody else. I'll get a job, I promise—"

"Okay, well, let's not worry about it now." Miri didn't want to break the news about children not being allowed to work. She opened her fist and looked at the delicate glass that lay in her palm. "I guess we'll just both have to look through it at the same time."

Molly nodded. "Maybe we should hold hands, too. For good measure." They joined hands, and Miri held up the little lens with her free hand. "Wait," Molly said a little anxiously. "Does it hurt?"

"Not really," said Miri. "It just feels weird, like you're sinking. But maybe going in this direction it'll feel like we're rising."

"Gosh. All right. I'm ready," said Molly firmly, as though saying she was would make it true.

"Me too. Put your head next to mine. There. Okay, now close your eyes and I'll hold up the glass. Open your eyes on the count of three."

"One," they said together. "Two. Three."

·⌒ CHAPTER ⌒·

5

THERE WAS NO WHIRLING, no dizzy sinking into the center of time, no nothing. Miri blinked. It had never occurred to her that it wouldn't work.

"Maybe the attic just looks the same in your time as it does in 1935," said Molly hopefully, glancing around the dusty space. "Maybe we did it, and we just don't know it."

Miri was doubtful. She hadn't felt a change, hadn't felt anything at all. But it was worth a try. "Maybe. Let's go back into your room and see if the wallpaper's purple."

They crept through the hinged door. It was much more awkward now that they weren't being chased, and the wooden flap banged down hard on Molly's knee. She folded her mouth into a line, but she didn't say anything. They emerged inside the closet and Miri saw at once that it was still 1935. She felt the first touch of panic wrinkling up her scalp. What if she couldn't get back home?

But Molly had another idea. "Maybe we just need to be in this room. Maybe that's part of the magic."

Miri was willing to try it. "Okay. Let's stand where I was when it happened." They positioned themselves on the rag rug and closed their eyes. Once again they peeked through the little glass on the count of three. Once again, the room and the year remained unchanged.

Molly saw the look on Miri's face. "Now, don't you worry," she said. "Don't fuss. Not yet." She paused and swallowed hard. "You go ahead. Maybe it's just for you."

"But you're the one who needs to get out of here," Miri argued.

"It's okay. It'll do, knowing that there's magic for real."

Miri stood holding the little glass. "I want to go, but I don't want to leave you here," she said helplessly.

Molly smiled, trying to look as if she didn't care. "Just go ahead, will you?"

So Miri did. But nothing changed. She lowered the lens from her eye and handed it to Molly. "Try it."

Without a word, Molly did, but it was useless. Her hand dropped to her side. They stared at each other; two eleven-year-old girls in the middle of a faded room in a big house on a country road in the year 1935.

.   .   .

Molly very kindly lent her a handkerchief. And then a second one, when the first got too soggy to be useful. She patted Miri's back, too, while she cried. But she didn't say anything dumb like It's not that bad or There's a silver lining to every cloud. Miri was grateful. She was stuck in 1935, and she would probably never see her mom and dad again, and nobody would believe her if she tried to explain what had happened, and she just had to cry. Every time she was about to stop, she would think something like "I'll never get to wear my purple boots again," and then she would start sobbing all over again. When she was finally all cried out and her skin was tight with dried tears, she rolled onto her back and looked at the familiar, peculiarly shaped ceiling. Molly, draped over the bed, was looking at the ceiling, too.

Miri tried to remember what she had learned in fifth-grade history. 1935. What was going on in 1935? Was it flappers and the Charleston? No, that's the twenties, she thought. Uh-oh. The Depression. The thirties were the Great Depression. "Great!" she moaned.

Molly looked at her with interest. It was the first non-sobbing noise she had made in a long time. "What?"

"1935! Right in the middle of the Great Depression! I have to get stuck in the Depression! Sheesh!"

"I never heard anybody call it 'great' before," said Molly.

"Great like big, not like terrific."

"Oh."

"Is everybody out of work? Are you poor and hungry?"

Molly laughed. "I'm hungry, but that's 'cause it's almost suppertime. I guess we're poor, but we're not as poor as some. Not like the Okies anyway. Flo's got a string of farms up and down the river."

But now Miri was remembering more. "Oh my God!"

Molly looked shocked. "You took the Lord's name in vain!"

"Sorry. I just remembered something."

"What?"

"There's a big war coming."

"What? When?" Molly yelped.

"In a few years. Right when we grow up," said Miri dismally.

"Between us and the Yankees again?" asked Molly.

"What? Oh. No. No, it doesn't happen here. It's mostly over in Germany and England and Japan, I think. But it's really big. What a bummer."

"What a what?"

"A bummer—a problem," explained Miri.

"I'm sorry I called you up from the future," apologized Molly.

"Oh, that's okay," said Miri. "I got to meet you, at least."

There was a silence. Miri lifted her feet in the air and looked at her sandals. She didn't even have any socks on, she observed. Trapped in 1935 without any socks. Mom wouldn't be happy about that. Oops. Don't think about Mom.

Molly, who was still holding the glass lens, dropped it over her right eye and squinted her eyebrow over it as if it were a monocle. "You know," she said.

After a second, Miri looked over to the bed. "You know what?"

"This glass," said Molly slowly. There was another silence.

"*What?*" said Miri. "What about it?"

"It's mine."

Miri sat up. "What do you mean?"

Molly remained draped over the bed, squinting through the glass. "It's mine. It's from my glasses."

"You don't have glasses," said Miri.

"Yes I do." Molly grinned. "I just lost 'em last week, and Aunt Flo says she ain't going to get me any more cause I lost the last pair, too." She made her voice sharp and shrill, "Just plain irresponsible, that's what it is, do you think we're made of money, there's a Depression going on, miss, in case you hadn't noticed it." She gave a snort and then fell back into her own voice, "But anyway, I don't know how I lost them. I was trying to take real good care of them 'cause Flo like to have a fit last time. I can't see more'n a couple feet away without glasses." She sighed, and then looked at the lens. "Too bad you just got the one. Where'd you find it again?"

"It was taped to the wall of my room. Your room. Just down there," said Miri, pointing at the wooden baseboard.

Molly stuck her index finger in her mouth and began to chew on it thoughtfully. "Wonder how it got there? Who put it there? And when?"

Miri felt her scalp wrinkle again, but this time her shivers didn't come from panic. This time they came from the spooky feeling that someone had taped the lens onto the wall of her room for a reason, someone who *knew* that the glass would take her back in time. The idea of magic had become somewhat less thrilling now that she couldn't get home, but Miri felt comforted by the thought that someone was guiding this adventure, that she was part of a plan instead of a freak accident.

Molly, pulling her finger out of her mouth, said, "Maybe it's spirits."

Spirits. Miri wrapped her arms around her knees. "You believe in ghosts, too?"

"Sure," said Molly with confidence. "Don't you?"

Miri rocked back and forth, thinking. "Yeah, I do. But not ghosts like most people think of them— spooks in sheets wandering around scaring people. I think they're more like echoes of people who aren't there anymore. You know?"

Molly turned her great gray eyes to Miri's. "Grandma May said something like that once. Back when she could talk, she said that some places can hold on to the past. In some places, everything that ever happened there is still happening, but just an echo of it." Molly smiled. "I didn't really under-stand what she was talking about, but maybe she was right. Maybe this is one of those places."

Miri stopped rocking. "Weird. Everything that ever happened is still going on?" She looked around the room. "Like if fifty years ago someone woke up in this room, that's still happening now?"

"Only ghost-like," said Molly solemnly. "Not solid-like."

There was a silence while they both thought about that.

"Kind of creepy," said Miri. "Now I feel like someone's breathing on me."

Molly giggled. "Give him a swat."

Miri batted the air. "Move aside," she said in a dignified way. "You're invading my personal space."

"Your what?" said Molly.

Before Miri could answer, the sharp clang of a bell sounded from below.

"Supper!" exclaimed Molly, jumping up from the bed. "Don't you fuss. I'm good at sneaking food. I'll bring you plenty."

"But aren't you going to get in trouble down there?" asked Miri uneasily. "Isn't Horst after you?"

"He never does anything real bad in front of his mama. She thinks he's a model boy, and he makes sure she keeps on thinking so." Molly gave a little smile. "'Sides, he's too busy stuffing his face to whop me. He don't put his fork down for anything. I'll be back soon." She slipped through the door, and Miri heard her steps patter away.

Miri looked around once more at the faded wallpaper. Trying to ignore her growling stomach, she inspected a small wicker bookshelf and found several tattered old friends. *Little Women, Eight Cousins,* and *Five Children and It*. She considered the fact that several of her favorite books would not be published for seventy more years. "Great," she muttered. "When I'm in my eighties, I'll find out what happens to Harry Potter."

Maybe she could even see her family then. But, her mind continued, maybe they won't know me. I wonder if I'm gone from their minds like I never existed or if it's like I just suddenly disappeared. The thought of them looking for her—calling her name in the woods, wondering where she could be, tears on her mother's cheeks, her father pale and worried—made Miri's stomach feel queasy again.

"I'm here," she whispered. "I'm here. I'll be fine." She didn't feel fine. She wanted her mother. She wanted to go home. She wanted it so much that it hurt. I have to get out of this room, she thought. I'm going to throw up if I stay in this room.

She opened the door as silently as she could. There was the narrow staircase and the hallway leading to the other bedrooms, just as they were in her own time. Summer-evening light drifted through the fan-shaped window above the landing. Miri descended the ladderlike stairs without one creak and ventured down the hall. A door stood slightly ajar, and through the gap Miri could see a dressing table with a ruffled skirt and a careful arrangement of glass perfume bottles set before a large mirror. That room must belong to Horst's sister, the one Molly called Sissy, thought Miri. What a goony name. I'd never let anyone call me Sissy.

Just as she always did, she brushed her fingertips along the smooth wood of the walls as she walked toward the large staircase that led to the first floor and felt the same surge of satisfaction that she was used to. The satiny surface was the same, the rooms were in the same places, and even the funny little gusts of cool air were the same. But it was definitely a different time. Nothing buzzed or beeped or rang. The air smelled less like cars and more like animals. Now she could hear voices and the clinking of forks against plates. Her stomach rumbled loudly, switching from queasy to hungry in a split second, and she wondered what would happen if she just walked into the dining room and demanded some food. Thinking of Horst, she decided against it.

She could hear him now, growling like her stomach. I wonder what he looks like, she thought. A bear, probably. She stood at the top of the stairs, hesitating. At the bottom was a large, square hallway—the same as in her time. Straight ahead was the front door, leading to the porch and the cool evening air beyond; on the left was the arched entrance to the dining room; and on the right was a twin arch leading to the living room. *If I can get into the living room,* Miri plotted, *I can sneak around to the kitchen and get a look at Horst through the hole in the sideboard.* She began to sidle down the stairs slowly, choosing moments when the conversation in the dining room would cover the random squawks of the wooden stairs.

A thin, whiney voice was complaining, ". . . *told* me it was on sale for seventeen cents a yard, but when I got there, it was twenty-one cents. Well, I said to her, Lottie, I guess it don't make much difference to me, but the one thing I don't care for . . ." As silent and agile as a spider, Miri glided down the stairs and turned into the living room.

There was only one problem. It was the dining room.

❧ CHAPTER ❧

6

FOR AN INSTANT, she faced them. They were so close, she could see them even without glasses. There was Aunt Flo, her black hair pulled sharply away from her face, her eyes on her plate, her long jaw moving in brisk, methodical jerks. Next was Sissy, a younger, prettier version of her mother with dark cropped hair and a floppy, brightly painted mouth. At her side was a bulky figure that had to be Horst. Molly said that he ate a lot, but even so, Miri was amazed by the size of him. His clothes seemed to stretch and strain to hold him in, and his wide legs threatened to crush the chair underneath him. His face was flat and flushed, and in his thick, meaty hands were a slab of bread and a chicken leg.

It was luck alone that kept them from seeing her. Luck and the fact that only Molly faced the doorway. She sat at the far end of the table, and at the moment Miri walked in the door, she happened to be gazing at the hallway, a view that was suddenly obstructed by the appearance of Miri. Miri saw her face freeze in horror; she saw that the others, interested only in their food and their complaints, had not noticed her; and she saw that they were about one second away from doing so.

Crash! Molly knocked her water glass to the floor. Miri whirled backward out of the room as the first sharp cries arose. Leaping out the front door, she heard the sound of a quick slap delivered to Molly's cheek and Aunt Flo's furious hiss, "Sloppy girl! Go get a towel—and pick up this glass! Do you have to break everything you touch, you worthless child?" Molly said nothing, but obediently scraped her chair back and trotted into the kitchen. With a pail and cloth, she returned and knelt to pluck the glass shards from the puddle of water.

"Hey, Mama," began Horst, giving Molly's back an unfriendly shove with his boot. "Do you reckon old Molly's got an allergic to glass? She broke this here cup today, and din't she lose her specs just last week?" Molly shot him a tense look, but he continued, "Seems like glass and her just don't get along." He grinned and took a giant bite off his chicken leg.

Her aunt glared at Molly. "She ain't got an allergy—she's just plain careless, is what. Can't be troubled to mind what she's doing. Can't be troubled to mind what it costs me. Molly Gardner thinks she's too important to pay attention to little things like money, I guess. Nothing's too good for Molly; anything our darling Molly wants—that's what your daddy always said. Wasn't it?" Molly, wiping water, kept her head down and did not reply.

"Well?"

"My father never said that," replied Molly in a low voice.

Her aunt's voice was higher and thinner than ever. "Don't tell fibs! Acting like you were a princess! Too bad for you that Pat Gardner never kept a promise in his life. Leaving you on my doorstep like a kitten. 'Just for a month, Flo,' he says. 'I'll be back in a month.' Should have known better than to listen to that man. Gone for good, and I'm stuck with you. Stuck with you." She spit the words.

"And you've never gotten a penny for her keep, have you, Ma?" asked Horst. Out on the front porch where she was crouched listening, Miri could hear the smile in his voice.

"Not a penny. For six years, I feed her, put clothes on her back, keep her in my own house—and what do I see from it?"

"Nothing," said Horst, sounding eager.

"Nothing," said Sissy, sounding bored.

Aunt Flo leaned back against her chair as if she was tired. "Well, it's too much. It surely is. It can't go on forever."

"What do you mean?" asked Molly quickly, looking up from her wiping.

Her aunt's face was cold and closed. "I'm not made of money," Flo snapped. "There's places for kids like you—kids whose parents run out on them. Nobody'd think twice if I took you down to the county and turned you over to the orphan institute. You can see how you like it there, miss. You won't be getting fancy new eyeglasses from them."

"Not much to eat, either," said Horst gleefully. "Those kids look like skeletons."

"They don't coddle 'em," said Flo. "Probably do her a world of good."

"Oh, Mother," sighed Sissy. "Really."

"Really, yourself," snorted Flo. "I mean to do it. One fine day in the near future . . ." Her voice drifted off as if she were in a lovely daydream.

"Hey, Molly," said Horst lazily. "I dropped my bread. Pick it up."

Molly picked up the bread and handed it to him in silence.

"Now wipe up that butter spot, girl. Just down there near my foot."

"Wipe up your own grease, Horst," said Molly quietly.

"What's that you say?" he choked, food spraying. "Did you hear her, Mama? Did you hear her sassing me? You'd better let me teach her a lesson, Mama—you'd better—" He stumbled over the words in his excitement

"You wipe up that butter, girl," said Flo, her voice deadly. "And then you can take your supper into the kitchen and eat it there. I don't want to see your face anymore."

Molly didn't reply. Miri heard her footsteps moving toward the kitchen door. As it closed behind her, Sissy mumbled, "She's not that bad, I don't think."

"She's bad enough," replied her mother. Then, louder, she called, "You'll be mopping the floor tonight to make up for breaking that glass. After the dishes."

Horst snickered.

. . .

Miri slipped quietly down the front stairs and around the side of the house. The sky was still light in the west, and she guessed it was around seven o'clock. Shadowy rhododendron bushes clustered against the side of the house and she heard the soft complaining sound of sleepy chickens nearby. Cautiously, she crept up the back steps and opened the porch door. The back porch was different from the one Miri knew; it was smaller and shakier, with a hulking item that looked like a giant meat grinder in one corner. Miri knew what it was: an old-fashioned washing machine. It looked like it ate arms, and she hoped that the automatic kind would be invented soon.

Having learned the lesson of the dining room, Miri peered carefully into the kitchen window before she entered. Squinting, she saw Molly at the sink, scrubbing a large black cooking pot with a rag. That was another thing that was a lot easier in her time. Too bad I didn't bring a Brillo pad along, thought Miri, watching Molly's arm pump up and down. Then she whispered, "Hey!"

The pot nearly slipped out of Molly's hands. "Oh my gosh!" she gasped. "You scared me!" She pulled Miri into the kitchen. "Why'd you go in the dining room? Golly Moses! I thought they were going to catch you for sure! I had to knock over that glass!"

"I'm sorry," said Miri earnestly. "In my house—or in my time, I guess I mean—that room is the living room. I didn't think your family would be eating in there. I'm really sorry I got you in so much trouble." Now that she was next to Molly, she could see that her eyes were red. "Your aunt and Horst are *horrible.*"

"Yeah," said Molly simply. She took a deep breath. "I'm going to run away."

"Jeez. I can see why," said Miri.

"And you should come with me." Molly's eyes were pleading.

Run away? Miri's eyes slid down to the floor and

then up to the sharp glare of the bare lightbulb that lit the kitchen. Suddenly, Miri realized something. She had been seeing Molly's life as something separate from hers. But it wasn't. Here in the world of 1935, Miri had a one-person family, and it was Molly. If she was going to grow up in this strange, unfamiliar world, she wanted to do it with Molly. What happened to Molly happened to her. "Okay," she said slowly. "I think I will." She gazed through the screened porch to the weathered barn. If she ran away, she would be leaving the last connection to her world. The only place that looked like home. But what good was it? It *wasn't* home; it only looked like it. And not even that much. And if they ran away, she wouldn't have to spend the rest of her life hiding from Horst and Aunt Flo. "Okay," she said again.

"You'll do it?" Molly exclaimed. "Oh, that's swell! I was afraid you wouldn't." She smiled hugely at Miri. "Here, let me make you some bread and butter. I didn't get to sneak any food from supper because of the glass." She turned busily from the sink to the countertop.

"Where are we going to run to?" asked Miri thoughtfully.

Molly hadn't figured that out. "I don't know yet. The woods, maybe?" She jerked her head to the dark trees beyond the barn.

"Hmm. What would we eat?" Miri asked. "You know how to trap animals?"

"No. Maybe I could learn. Or we could eat berries—but not in the winter, I guess. I heard New York City is nice," said Molly. "My daddy sent me a postcard from there once. Hey! Maybe we could find my daddy and live with him."

"Maybe." Miri remembered pictures she had seen of people selling apples on street corners during the Depression. "Might be kind of hard to get to New York City, though. Unless—do you have any money?"

"Ha! Any money I get, *she* takes it." Molly handed her a generous slice of bread, slathered with butter.

Miri took a large bite and tried to think. The magic had brought her here—maybe they would magically find money if they ran away. Maybe. Probably not. Running away without any money in the middle of the Depression didn't seem like a very good plan.

"I got an idea where I can get some money,

though," said Molly, her eyes bright and determined. Miri thought that this was probably how she looked when she sawed the passageway into the attic.

"Where?"

"I'll steal it!"

"How?"

Molly grinned. "From Horst. He's got loads of money stashed away somewhere. I know he does, but I don't know where. I've been searching his room when he's not home, but he's such a loafer he spends half the day on that dumb bed."

"How come you think he's got money?" asked Miri. "I mean, where would he get it if he doesn't work?"

Molly looked over her shoulder and then leaned her head toward Miri's. "He's a thief," she said in a low voice.

"A thief?" Miri, chewing, was doubtful. "I thought thieves were supposed to be smart. Why do you think so?"

"For one, he's always got money. Nobody round-about here has much money, but Horst always has a big roll of greenbacks in his pocket," Molly explained excitedly, looping one of her crooked braids over her ears. "Not that he gives his ma or his sister any, but I seen him take it out at the store to get his own stuff. And second, there was a bunch of things getting stolen in Paxton last winter, and when I went to town in June I heard from Mrs. Baker—you know what's funny? She works in the bakery—she said that Judge Kent's house got robbed and the robber took Mrs. Kent's pink gold bracelet." Molly ran out of breath, and looked at Miri in triumph, as though she had proved that Horst had done it.

But Miri was looking absently at the sink, where the dishes sat forgotten in gray water. She was remembering what Ray and Robbie had told her, was it only that morning? It seemed like years ago. An old man, who had lived in the valley for a long time, had said that there was stolen jewelry buried on their property. A thief had once lived in the house, but none of his loot had ever been found. Maybe it was Horst. He was crummy and nasty enough to be a criminal, that was for sure. But he's such a loser, she thought. He'd get caught in a minute. What if he's just pretending to be a loser? This was a worrying thought, and Miri was about to share it with Molly, when a sharp voice called from the dining room. "Those dishes had better be done!" Both girls recognized the tight crack of heels against the floor.

"Barn!" hissed Molly.

With an agonized nod, Miri leaped toward the back door—and slammed full-speed into the kitchen table. A frying pan the size of a wheel crashed to the floor with a thunderous clatter. "Sorry!" Miri managed to whisper as she flung herself out the door.

Not a minute too soon. Flo whirled in furiously. "You worthless, stupid girl!" she raged. "Are you possessed by the devil? Wouldn't surprise me, not atall. Or maybe you're *trying* to destroy my house. Is that it? I wouldn't put it past you for a minute, not a minute! Ohh." She knelt to pick up the vast pan, and rubbed her hands over the floor. "You took a big chunk out of the wood here. And don't tell me you didn't mean to—I know you! I'll teach you about clumsy, miss!"

Meanwhile, Miri threw herself down the back steps into the soft blue night and landed with a thump in a bed of dirt. There was the barn, looming ahead of her, a dark shape against the sky. She headed toward it through a cloud of lightning bugs. At least lightning bugs in summer were the same.

She could hear Flo's harsh voice scolding Molly about the frying pan, and some soft music from a radio deep inside the house. Miri edged closer to the rhododendron bushes for cover.

Suddenly, the faded evening was pierced by two bright beams. A truck creaked down the dirt drive by the side of the house, its headlights glaring over the grass, the elm, and the tired gray boards of the barn. Miri cringed and backed herself into the nearest bush until she had fully disappeared. She heard a car door slam and mild, shuffling steps moving toward the back door. A meek knock, and Flo stuck her head out the window. "Who's there?"

"It's Bud, ma'am. Sissy at home?"

"Whyn't you come to front door, Bud?" asked Flo crabbily. "We've got one."

"Yes, ma'am," the voice agreed. "Do you want me to go around?"

"Siss-*y!*" hollered Flo. "Bud Water's here at the back door."

Miri heard a window open. "Why on earth do you have to come to the back door like a cracker?" said Sissy. "I must have told you a hundred times."

"I forgot," said Bud. "I'm sorry."

"Go out to the front." The window slammed. The meek footsteps shuffled away.

Miri had a sudden vision of Sissy at about age fifty. She would be just exactly as mean as her mother. She's only a little nice now because she's young and pretty, thought Miri. Feeling intelligent, she climbed out of the rhododendron bush and walked quickly to the barn, pulling leaves out of her hair.

᪲ CHAPTER ᪲

7

MIRI'S EYES CLICKED open. She lay very still, trying to figure out where she was. As her eyes adjusted to the dim light, she saw rough wooden boards rising over her head. Her hand cautiously patted the floor beneath her. What was this stuff? She brought some of it close to her face. Hay. The barn. She was hiding in the barn—and now it all came pouring and tumbling back, like water out of a faucet. She sat up and shivered in the nighttime cool. Where was Molly? And what time was it? And how long had she been sleeping?

She had come up into the loft because it seemed to offer better hiding opportunities. Down below, in the regular part of the barn, there was a dopey-looking cow in a stall and a lot of rusty machinery. There were also chickens in a coop just outside, and for a moment she had thought of stowing away there, but then she realized that the chickens would probably freak out, and besides, she didn't want to be that close to chickens. They gave her the creeps.

The cow stared at her stupidly while Miri pondered. Then she saw the ladder leading up into the darkness above. A loft—that was just exactly what she needed! Up she climbed, and the first thing she saw was a big, puffy stack of hay. In a moment, she was comfortably stretched out on top of it.

She would just rest for a while, she thought, until Molly showed up. But her eyes kept closing, and her brain, trying to make sense of the day, stumbled and looped until it was whirling with shovels and glasses and a small iron bed and a cat (where was the cat?) and Molly's braids and fairies and Aunt Flo's pinched nose and Horst's meaty hand closing over a chicken leg and Molly's smile when she said, "I'll steal it!" And where was Molly anyway?

After a few minutes of struggling, sleep won. Miri's eyes fell shut and she dreamed she was in a house of mirrors with her brothers and they wanted to break all the mirrors. "You can't do that!" cried Miri indignantly. "No one will be able to see themselves!"

She was so mad she woke up.

Now, listening in the dark loft, she became aware of a sound from below. It was a quiet scraping, the sort of sound you make if you're trying not to let people hear you. There's Molly! thought Miri eagerly. Molly must be creeping around, looking for her.

Miri leaned forward to call to her friend but a little whisper of caution stopped her. She remembered the dining room disaster and thought, Look first. So she leaned out from the loft to peer into the barn below, expecting to see Molly scuffling about with her crooked braids and limp dress.

The barn was dim, its corners lost in shadows. But even in the half-light, Miri could see that the figure below did not belong to Molly. It was Horst. He was kneeling on the wooden floorboards near a high wagon, his wide back toward Miri, and, by the light of a small lantern, he was carefully, gently pulling up one of the boards in the floor. Miri couldn't believe how quiet he was being.

She held her breath. What if she sneezed? Her

arms began to itch, but she didn't dare to move them. She didn't dare move any part of herself, because being caught by Horst was the worst thing she could imagine. Frozen, she watched him, pulling ever so carefully until the board came free. He put it aside and reached his short arm deep beneath the floor, grunting quietly with the effort. Then he pulled out a black box, about the size of a shoe box, but made of metal.

At least Miri thought it was made of metal. It had a shiny surface, but she couldn't see very well in the dim light. She stared at Horst, first squinting and then opening her eyes wide, trying to force them to see clearly. Horst fumbled in his pocket for something—a key, she guessed—and unlocked the box. It was so still in the barn that she could hear the click of the lock turning. Horst gave a little wheeze of pleasure as he looked at the box's contents—and Miri gave a soft huff of impatience. If only she could see. She squeezed her eyes into slivers and caught the quick gleam of something like glass—or jewels!

This was what Molly had been talking about: Horst's secret stash. And it looked like she had been right about him being a thief. Why else would he be keeping jewels hidden in the barn? Assuming they actually were jewels. If only she could see better! Miri wiggled with frustration and strained forward on her stomach to get a better view.

As she did so, a hard lump in her pocket pressed painfully into her thigh. Ow. She reached into the pocket, and her fingers touched the familiar frames of her glasses. The ones that Ray had broken that afternoon.

Silently, she pulled them out for inspection. One frame was bent and the glass had cracked across one lens, but they'd work well enough to let her see what Horst was hiding. She had to press her hand over her mouth to keep from giggling. Wait till I tell Molly, she thought, slipping the bent arms over her ears. She closed one eye and, with the other, looked through the unbroken lens.

A cold wind blew through the cracks in the barn roof, and the rough boards of the barn seemed to wobble and bend. "Oh no!" cried Miri, wildly pulling off her glasses and hurling them away. "Not now!" She could just make out Horst's face, startled, looking up, before he seemed to melt like wax, and she was being pulled up, up, through the center of time, while the barn and Horst and the wavering shadows fell away behind her.

. . .

"No!" Frantically, Miri rolled over and began to claw at the earth beneath her, as though she could dig herself back in time. "No, no, *no* . . ." Her voice trailed off as she realized how ridiculous her efforts were. Ridiculous. She sat back on her knees and sobbed with frustration and misery. She couldn't leave *now.* Not yet, not without Molly. Molly would think Miri had abandoned her. Molly would be all alone again, alone in the world with her rotten aunt—and Horst.

Miri sucked her breath in sharply. Horst. He wasn't just creepy and mean; he was a criminal, a real-life criminal. Miri groaned. Molly had no idea how dangerous her situation was, and there was no way Miri could tell her. "Don't mess with Horst," she whispered. Miri pictured Molly lying in her little white bed, waiting to sneak out to the barn, and she tried to send a telepathic message through time: *Stay where you are.*

Wiping away the tears on her cheeks, Miri lay down on a damp clump of weeds and looked at the starry night sky above her. She was home. She was back in her very own time, in her very own backyard. A few hours ago, it was all she had wanted. But now everything was different. It wasn't right without Molly. It's like when Mom gets sick, Miri thought. Something's missing; something isn't right. She sighed and glanced toward the leggy black shadows of the blackberry branches jutting into the sky. They marked the spot where the far end of the barn had been. At least, Miri reflected, the magic hadn't dropped her from the height of the loft to the ground. The fall would have broken one of her legs, probably both.

But maybe I didn't fall down, she thought. Maybe I was pushed up. That was what it had felt like. Slowly, Miri got to her feet and brushed off her dress. Oops. The magic hadn't taken such good care of her glasses—they lay where she had flung them, and now *both* lenses were cracked clean across. Miri plucked them from the dust and peered at them in the moonlight. They looked like ordinary broken glasses. How could they send her through time?

Miri turned toward her house, which stood quiet and welcoming in the night. Despite its extra rooms and staircases, it looked solid, as though it would always be there. Lightning bugs gleamed briefly in the darkness and then disappeared in the warm stream of light that flowed from the kitchen window. Miri could see a blurry figure moving around the room. It was her mother. She felt a sudden, sharp ache—happy to be home, sorry that Molly wasn't—and walked swiftly up the porch stairs to the kitchen door. Before she could begin to worry about explaining where she had been or what had happened, her mother looked up from the counter where she was working and opened her arms.

WHEN SHE FINALLY REALIZED what her mother was saying, Miri almost laughed.

". . . an imagination is a wonderful thing, Miri, and I don't want you to think that I don't appreciate yours. You've got a beautiful, rich world in that brain of yours." Her mother stroked Miri's forehead softly. "But baby, you've got to understand that you don't live in that imaginary world. You live in the real one, and it's much more complicated and, well—dangerous—than I'd like it to be." She looked at Miri searchingly, and for one wild moment Miri thought her mother was telling her that it was all a dream, that Molly and her world were just made up.

"But Mom! You weren't there! You can't know—"

"I do know, sweetie," her mother broke in soothingly. "You were very angry—and we need to talk about that, too—but honey, running away is not a solution. I know you read about it in books and it sounds exciting, but in the real world, it's a bad idea. That's why children have parents to take care of them—because the world is a crazy place."

"Running away?" said Miri blankly.

Her mother squeezed her shoulders and said, "I know you didn't mean to scare me. Your father said I should call the police, but I felt sure you'd be back in a few hours, and I didn't want to get the police involved."

That was when Miri almost laughed. Her mother thought she had run away. The idea was hilarious. She *had* been on the verge of running away—from Flo and Horst. But actually, all she had wanted the whole time was to run home, bringing Molly with her. She was about to tell her mom the whole story. In fact, she opened her mouth to say, Don't worry, I didn't run away. But she quickly shut it again.

How could she explain? Miri knew with certainty that her mother would never believe in Molly, in time traveling, in any of it. She would think Miri was bonkers and take her to a psychiatrist, who would also think she was bonkers. After a while, Miri herself might come to believe she was bonkers. And that would be the end of magic. Miri remembered the wonderful warm feeling of learning that magic was real and that it had happened to her and Molly. That was hers. If she kept the magic a secret, that feeling would be hers forever, even if it never happened again.

So she adjusted her face and tried to look pitiful. "I'm sorry," she said. "I didn't mean to worry you. It was just so unfair that I got blamed for hitting Ray when he started it all. And he broke my glasses, too." She sniffed in a pathetic way.

Her mother hugged her again. "I know," she murmured. "I know. Let's talk about it."

. . .

They talked for nearly an hour, and then her mother called her father, and Miri had to talk to him, too. He told her that he understood why she had hit Ray, but that controlling her temper was an important life skill and . . . After a while, Miri stopped listening. They were being very nice, especially considering how hard she had whacked her brother on the head, but she couldn't wait to escape to her bedroom.

When she finally entered her room, Miri glanced immediately toward the dark corner where she had found the glass lens that afternoon. Of course, she knew it couldn't be there, because it was somewhere in Molly's world, maybe in her pocket or something, but she had a hope that somehow the magic would let it reappear. Instead, the wood board was smooth and empty, holding nothing. The disappointment was like a weight dropping on her. Why couldn't you just let it *be* there? she demanded and instantly apologized. She had read enough stories to know that magic punished the ungrateful. "Thank you," she said out loud, stretching her face into a wide, fake smile. Sheesh, she thought after a moment, maybe I *am* bonkers. No, she knew she wasn't. And besides, she missed Molly. Who misses an imaginary person?

Miri slipped into her closet and flicked on the light. Her own clothes hung unevenly on their hangers, looking out of place. Miri knelt on the untidy pile of shoes on the floor and pulled up the lid of the long, low bench. Yes—it rose with a resentful squeal. I am such a dork, thought Miri. I never even checked it before. She peered inside. Maybe she would find a clue, something that belonged to Molly, something that would prove that Molly was real and that Miri had really met her that afternoon.

At first glance, it, too, was a bust. There were a few frayed, no-color ribbons at one end. There was a glass jar containing the remains of several spiders. There was a single brown shoe with a hole in the toe. There was bunch of cloth violets that probably didn't look very good even when they were new. And there was a stack of magazines. The secret flap that led to the attic had been nailed shut from the other side. Miri saw little nail points jutting through the wood. She thumped her fist against the boards, but they didn't budge. Miri was about to close the bench when it occurred to her that the magazines might be interesting. She pulled the pile out and began to leaf through them. They were all from the thirties and forties: *Life, Saturday Evening Post, Motion Picture,* and *Ladies' Home Journal.* At any other time, Miri would have liked looking at the pictures, but now she tossed them to the floor impatiently.

A thin paper notebook with a blue cover slid out

from the pages of a *Saturday Evening Post*. Miri opened it, her hands trembling with excitement. "Molly Gardner" was written in flowing cursive in the right-hand corner of the first page. Wow, her handwriting is a lot nicer than mine, thought Miri. Below, where the lines began, a date was tidily noted: September 4, 1934. "Fifth grade began. Miss Dilys Fanning. Cow out. Nothing." Immediately below on the next line was "September 5, 1934. Reading good. Laundry. Nothing." On the next line, "September 6, 1934. Multiplication tables. Made black-berry muffins. Nothing." Miri frowned as her eyes ran down the page. What was "Nothing"? And why bother to write at all if you weren't going to say any more than that? She flipped a page: "Nothing . . . Nothing . . . Nothing . . ." It was at the end of every entry. She flipped another page, and another, until she came to the last entry: "July 22, 1935. Miri came." The rest of that page and all the following pages were blank.

The notebook fell from Miri's hands, and she stared wide-eyed at the white wall before her. It *had* all happened. The magic was real. She had gone back in time that afternoon and met an eleven-year-old girl named Molly. The last tiny doubt disappeared from her mind like a popping soap bubble, and a question arose to fill the newly cleared space: Why? Why had it happened? And why had the magic chosen her?

Miri was pretty sure that it was not because she was good. Cinderella, for example, now *she* was good: singing while she cleaned the house, happily sewing for her nasty stepsisters. And that's why her fairy godmother had given her the coach, the dress, the prince. Miri had always found Cinderella annoying, but she was definitely better than Miri. Miri complained if she had to clean even her own room. And look at this afternoon—she had almost killed Ray with a shovel. No, the magic hadn't chosen her because she was good.

Despite what Molly had said, Miri was also positive she wasn't a fairy. Or a witch. She had never once talked to an animal. Or flown. She would have noticed.

There was only one other reason that she could think of. She had been chosen—or called up, like Molly said—because she was supposed to do something helpful. She was supposed to solve a problem.

Miri rubbed her finger across the smooth blue cover of Molly's notebook. Molly had a problem, all right, and its name was Horst. Aunt Flo was a meanie, but there was something about Horst—Miri saw his thick, angry face turning toward her in the barn, and shook herself like a dog shaking off water. Yuck. She couldn't stand to think of Molly being in the same house with him. She flipped through the notebook until she reached the last entry. "Miri came," she read. But that wasn't good enough. "I've got to get her out of there," she muttered. Miri took a long, slow breath. All right, then. If she was supposed to save Molly, she'd be happy to do it.

But how?

Miri dropped her head into her hands and began to think.

. . .

About an hour later, Miri was sitting at her desk with Molly's notebook opened before her. At the top of a blank page, she wrote "Possibilities. 1. Best: I figure out how to go back to 1935 and return with Molly." Miri tapped her pen against her teeth and looked at what she had written. The best seemed to require a lot of luck. *How* was she going to go back to 1935? Not to mention returning—with Molly—to her own time? The magic did not seem inclined to whisk them back and forth just because they wanted it to.

Think logically, she told herself sternly. What do you already know about the magic? She smiled; when Miri or Robbie or Ray asked their father for help with their homework, he always began by saying, "What do you already know?" about frogs, or Cherokee Indians, or Egyptian mummies, or whatever they were working on. What did she already know? Not a thing. She looked through an eyeglass lens and ended up in 1935. She looked through another one and ended up at home. Miri sighed and wrote "Glasses."

Wait, though. She also knew that it was her own glasses that had brought her home. How could her own glasses be magic? They were just her glasses, glasses that she had worn every day for the last six months, not like the mysterious lens taped to her wall, the one that had taken her to Molly. What had she thought when she looked through it? *Whoever owned this must have really bad eyesight.* But that wasn't true, because Molly had said that the lens was exactly like hers, and her eyes hadn't seemed so bad.

No. That's not what Molly had said. She had said that the lens *was* hers.

Miri let out a grunt of surprise, and then pressed her hand to her forehead as though she could squeeze the memory out. Molly had been lying on the bed, with the old glass lens over her eye like a monocle. "It's mine," she had said.

So there it was. The glasses that took her there were Molly's. The glasses that brought her home were hers. Molly's glasses let her look into Molly's world. Miri's would let Molly come into hers. Of course. That's why nothing had happened when they looked through the little glass in Molly's attic— they were already there. Each lens was a one-way ticket to the other time, a tiny glass time machine. Her regular old glasses had turned into a time machine. It couldn't last, Miri reasoned. That would be too much to ask. The glasses would be magic only long enough to bring Molly home. Only long enough for Miri to do what she was supposed to do. Molly's glasses would take her to 1935. Her glasses would bring them home. Okay.

The next step was simple. All she had to do was find a pair of Molly's glasses.

The next step was impossible. How was she going to find a pair of Molly's glasses?

"I'll look everywhere," she promised in a whisper. But what good would that do? People didn't just leave glasses lying around for eighty years. But maybe she could find the pair that Molly had lost. Maybe Molly had shoved them to the back of some drawer or closet by mistake, and they were lying there, waiting. After all, she reminded herself, lost stuff has to be *somewhere*. "I'll find them," she said firmly, but inside she was doubtful. Maybe, she thought hopefully, any pair from 1935 would do. Maybe I can just buy some antique glasses and get back there.

Miri yawned hugely and squinted at her clock. To her surprise, it said 1:43. Wow. This was the latest she had ever stayed up. What a day. She turned the page over and wrote "Things to Do" at the top. "1. Look for Molly's glasses. 2. Buy 1935 glasses." Miri yawned again. "3. Get new glasses for me." The unbroken lens was the one that had lifted her out of the barn; she didn't think that they'd work now that both sides were smashed. And besides, she couldn't see.

She read her list, trying to ignore the voice that was whispering, *What if you can't find Molly's glasses? What if you can't get back? What if you had your chance and blew it?* "Shut up!" Miri said aloud. She stood up and stretched. Her bed was smooth and comfortable looking, and Miri threw herself facedown on the familiar yellow quilt and closed her eyes. Ahh. She was so tired. Without opening her eyes she reached up to turn out the lamp. Sleep. Sleep.

But sleep did not come. There was a worry prodding her mind, and it was like trying to walk with a blister on her heel. *Go away,* she said to her mind. But the worry kept poking and rubbing and nudging. It wouldn't let her alone. After a long time, Miri got up and went to her desk.

She snapped on the light and grimly turned the page over again, back to "Possibilities." She picked up her pen and wrote, "2. Bad: Molly runs away before I can get back." She thought for a moment and wrote, "3. Worst: I never get back at all." She hesitated for a moment and returned to bed. But there was something even worse than that, so bad that she didn't want to write it down. She couldn't stop herself from imagining it, though. 4. Horst lumbering to his feet, his face purple with fury, his bellow rising to a scream as he thunders up to the loft. *"You're going to be sorry now, runt! You're going to wish you was never born!"* Horst kicking savagely at the hay, hoping to connect with bone and finding nothing. Horst raging that his victim had escaped yet again, his heavy boots grinding the old wooden ladder rungs, his breath coming in grunts as he runs into the house, rushes up the narrow staircase, and throws his meaty shoulder against the door until it shivers open. Molly, startled, sitting up in bed, her face white and scared. And Horst smiling—

Stop. I don't want to think this anymore, Miri pleaded with her mind. She rolled over and burrowed her face into her pillow. *Stop.* But her mind wouldn't stop. She pictured all of the empty pages after July 22, 1935. What had happened on July 23?

MIRI HAD DECIDED to wake at the break of dawn to begin her search for a pair of Molly's glasses, but dawn came and went, and Miri slept on. When she finally opened her eyes, she found Nell and Nora peering at her silently, their hot little faces nearly touching hers. It was their favorite way to wake her up.

"Go away!" groaned Miri. "I must have told you a thousand times not to do that."

"We didn't do anything," Nell said, climbing into the bed.

"We're the quietmost sisters," Nora nodded, grabbing hold of Miri's nightgown and pulling her way under the covers.

"Oh, let go of it, Nora. You'll rip it."

"You let me in," commanded Nora.

"Okay, okay." Miri rolled into the center of the bed to make room for her sisters and they snuggled against her, one little blond head on each side.

"Mommy says we're supposed to be nice to you," offered Nell. She kissed Miri's arm. It tickled.

"Mommy says we're not good enough when you take care of us, but I am," said Nora.

"I am, too," said Nell confidently.

Miri giggled. They were pretty cute sometimes.

"Even though you hit Ray with a shovel, he has to be nice to you, too. Mommy said," announced Nora.

"And Robbie, too. But he says he's not going to. Don't tell Mommy."

"And Mommy says when Daddy comes home, she's going to take you to the beach, just you and Mommy," Nora said, proud of all her information. "And we can't go. And Daddy will have to take care of us."

Miri looked at her sister. "She said that?"

Nell and Nora nodded together.

"When's Daddy coming home?"

The two girls replied with identical shrugs. Miri sat up. She didn't want to go to the beach with her mother—well, she did, but not yet. First she had to get back to Molly. "Get up, kids," she said, throwing back her sheet. "I've got to get busy." Her sun-shaped clock informed her that it was ten in the morning. "Jeez," she muttered. "It's late."

Miri clattered downstairs, leaving Nell and Nora in her bed arguing over which one was a kitty. She planned to grab something to eat and begin her search for Molly's glasses immediately, but when she got to the kitchen her mother was standing at the stove. "Hi, bunny!" she called. "I'm making you some French toast!"

Most of the time Miri loved French toast, but this morning it was just another obstacle to her plans. Still, she thought, looking at her mother's cheerful face, there's a lot to be said for staying on Mom's good side. So she smiled gratefully, sat down at the kitchen table, and munched her way through two enormous slices of French toast and an orange. Chew and swallow, chew and swallow.

"Now, Miri, what would you like to do today?" asked Mom.

Miri gulped. "Um, Mom? This morning I think I'm going to do some work getting my room the way

I want it." She knew that her mother loved any plan that began with *I'm going to do some work,* and sure enough, her mother beamed. "And this afternoon maybe we could go get me some new glasses?" She blinked in what she hoped was a pathetic way.

"That sounds good, honey." Her mom smiled extra enthusiastically. "While we're in town, we can go to the paint store and pick out some paint for your room. And Miri, when Daddy gets home next Tuesday, I thought you and I could take a little trip down to Cape Romain. Just the two of us."

Miri smiled and nodded with as much excitement as she could muster. Boy, Mom must be feeling guilty—but why? "That'll be great," she said, swallowing the last lump of French toast. Now the orange. Under the table, her bare feet bounced impatiently against the wooden floor, eager to get moving. "Mom?" she began. "Was there any—" She broke off, surprised.

"Any what?" her mother prompted.

But Miri had forgotten her question. Her big toe had stumbled from the smooth surface of the floor into a wide crack. What? Miri stuck her head under the table and saw a deep canyon in the wood, smooth-edged from years of wear. Somehow, a long time before, a big chunk of the floor had been gouged out.

By a frying pan, falling heavily from a table.

"Miri?" Mom said anxiously as Miri failed to emerge from under the table.

Miri came back up, wide-eyed. The chip was right under Miri's usual seat at the table. She certainly would have felt it before—if it had been there. "Was this floor always chipped?" she asked, hoping her voice wasn't squeaky.

"What?" Her mother stared at her, obviously surprised by her daughter's sudden interest in kitchen floors.

"This deep crack," said Miri, pushing back her chair to show her mother the gouge in the wood.

Her mother began explaining, "All the floors on the bottom story could use some work, and it would have been nice if we could have refinished them before we moved in, but—"

Miri interrupted, "Mom! Are you saying that you've seen this chip in the floor before?"

"Miri! That was so rude."

Miri took a breath. "Mom," she said as politely as

she could manage, "please, was this chip in the floor when you bought the house?"

"Yes, the chip was there. That's what I'm trying to tell you—we wanted to refinish the floors before we moved in, but it's a terrible mess because the dust . . ."

Miri wasn't listening. The chip hadn't been there until yesterday. It hadn't been there seventy years before yesterday either. But since yesterday, it had been there for seventy years. Miri stood up abruptly. "Great!" she said, giving her mother a big, toothy smile. "Okay! Thanks for the delicious French toast, Mom." She whisked out of the kitchen.

"—and we decided we didn't have enough time," concluded Mom, to herself.

. . .

Miri stared into her own green eyes in the bathroom mirror. In 1935, she had banged into a kitchen table, knocking over a frying pan and denting the wooden floor. And now, in her own time, the floor was dented in that precise spot, but the crack was worn with age. Even though it hadn't been there the day before.

This is too weird, thought Miri. I changed the house. I changed history.

But the weirdest thing of all was that her mom thought the crack had always been there.

I changed Mom's history, too.

Her hair brushed against her cheek, and a long shiver twitched along Miri's spine. What if I changed Molly's history, too—for the worse? She thought of Aunt Flo's furious voice saying, "I'll teach you about clumsy, miss!" She thought of Horst, choking with excitement, "You'd better let me teach her a lesson, Mama—you'd better—" With an effort, Miri pulled her eyes away from the mirror. She had to find Molly's glasses—and quick.

· · ·

"Mom? Was there any old furniture in the house when we moved in?"

Her mother looked up from the computer. "What's got into you? Floors, furniture—are you planning a career in interior decoration?"

"No. I just wanted to know if there was old furniture in the house when we moved in," Miri repeated.

"You were here when we moved in," Mom pointed out. "Did you see any old furniture?"

"Um, I guess I wasn't paying very much attention," admitted Miri. "Was there? Like a desk? With drawers?"

"Not that I know of. There was a tool chest in the basement, but that's all." She glanced at her computer screen. "Why?"

"I kind of like old furniture," Miri said. It wasn't a lie. She did. "I thought if there was some, I could put it in my room."

"Oh," said her mother. "You should probably wait until after we take down that nasty wallpaper and put on some paint before you think about . . . about . . ." Her voice trailed off as her eyes slipped back to the computer.

"Candy bars," said Miri, rolling her eyes.

"Right," Mom mumbled. "Candy bars."

Miri left the room.

"What?" she heard her mother say.

• • •

Start with the tool case, Miri decided. She squeezed between the stacks of cardboard boxes that lined the pantry and pulled open the basement door. Dying screams split the air; her brothers were listening to their music. They were also arguing.

"Dude! It's cement! How would he get it under cement, unless he's, like, a superhero?" Robbie shouted over the howls.

"Maybe he buried it and then put the cement over it to keep it safe—did you ever think of that?" Ray bellowed.

The stairs creaked as Miri descended. "Hi."

Her brothers stopped talking abruptly. She thought they would still be mad at her, but they didn't look mad. And they didn't look like they had never seen her before, which was how they usually looked. They looked . . . uneasy. "Hi," they said in unison.

The three of them looked at one another. Ray turned off the CD player. "Uh, I'm sorry I chased you and knocked you down and broke your glasses and all that."

"Yeah, me too," said Robbie.

Miri stared at them. Boy, Mom must have gone completely off her nut, she thought. This had never happened before. "I'm sorry I hit you on the head," she said. "Does it still hurt?"

"Yeah. A little." Ray gave her a flashing smile. "Got a big lump." He lifted his brown hair and pointed.

Miri couldn't see anything, but she didn't want to seem unsympathetic. "Wow. I'm sorry."

" 'Sokay," Ray said.

They looked at one another in awkward silence.

"Did Mom freak?" Miri asked at last.

Robbie and Ray both broke into grins. "Totally ballistic," said Robbie.

"Out of her freaking mind," added Ray. "I'm sitting there with a concussion probably, because *you* hit *me,* and she's mad at me. She's saying we gang up on you and never include you, yada yada yada. And you've just tried to kill me! Whoa! Reality check!" he snorted. "Plus, she's totally out to lunch, 'cause we do too include you, all the time." Robbie nodded.

"Oh, right. Like helping you look for the stolen stuff," said Miri sarcastically.

There was a surprised silence. Then Robbie said, "You wanna help us dig?"

Ray shot him a look. "Dude."

"She can if she wants," said Robbie. "We haven't found anything yet."

Miri looked at the piles of dirt scattered around

the basement floor. It looked like they were trying to dig sideways underneath the cement floor. She considered telling them that they were looking in the wrong place, that the stuff was out in the backyard where the barn used to be. But Molly might need to find Horst's stash so she could run away. Might have needed it? Miri didn't know how to think about time anymore. Were things that hadn't happened yet in the past actually in the future? It was too confusing.

"No, thanks," she replied after a moment. "I'm working on another project—" She broke off, realizing that for the first time in her life, she didn't care whether she was included. She wasn't mad at them, and she didn't feel disappointed or left out. Getting Molly was more important. She grinned at her brothers, and after a moment they grinned back at her.

"Have you guys seen an old tool chest down here?" she asked.

"Tool chest? Nah." Robbie flicked on the CD player again, and yowls filled the room. "Wish we had an iPod."

"That's why we gotta keep digging," said Ray, picking up a shovel. "We need money."

"Sounds like they're hitting each other with their guitars," said Miri.

"They are," said Ray, climbing over the short wall that separated the cement floor from the dirt part of the basement. "It's Deathbag." He glanced at her blank face. "You must've heard of them." Miri shook her head. "They're totally awesome. 'Kay, bro," he called to his brother. "Hand me the shovel. You hold the flashlight."

Miri turned away. Digging underneath a cement slab didn't look like much fun. Why had she wanted so much to be part of it? And if they did succeed in digging under the floor, her dad was going to be pretty mad. But she wasn't going to interfere. Live and let live. She peered into the dim corners of the basement. There were some old shelves on one wall. All empty. Was that a workbench? She took a few steps toward it. Yes, with an old pegboard above it, and below—she knelt and stuck her head underneath the high table, trying to catch a glimmer of light in the darkness. And there it was. A tool chest. Or at least a big dirty box. Miri reached through the cobwebs and dragged it into better light.

At the sound of the box scraping against the

floor, Robbie and Ray looked up. "Hey!" Ray said. "What'd you find?"

"A tool chest," she said, kneeling beside it.

"How come you found it and not us?" asked Ray, climbing back over the wall for a better look.

" 'Cause you're goons," replied Miri, yanking on the latch that held the lid down. It was stuck. "Also, Mom told me it was here."

"I got it," said Robbie, squatting down next to her. He jabbed his shovel under the latch and slammed down with his fist.

The rusty metal abruptly gave way, and Miri pulled the lid up with eager hands. There was a hammer dark with age and a collection of bent nails. But maybe at the back—there could be a pair of glasses stuck in the back! Miri plunged her hand into the box, feeling against the darkness.

Nothing. Nothing, nothing, nothing.

Miri sat back on her heels and tried not to be miserable. The voice in her brain began its gloomy recitation: *You are never going to find a pair of Molly's glasses.* Molly *couldn't even find her glasses. This is never going to work.* Shut up, she told it. I've got to try. *Seventy-five-year-old glasses. Sure. No problem.* Her brain was sassing her. Shut *up*, she thought, and stood. "You want this hammer?" she asked Robbie.

"Huh?" said Robbie. "Oh. Sure. Thanks."

"We could sort of scrape against the bottom of the cement," Ray said.

"Yeah," said Robbie.

"Except we can't find the bottom of the cement," Ray went on.

They went back to the other side of the basement and Miri went back up the creaking stairs. The bright sunlight in the kitchen made her blink. She moved through the house, trying to look at each room like she was seeing it for the first time. She was rewarded by noticing a worn wooden garland carved into the mantel over the fireplace. And the dots on the faded dining room wallpaper were actually grapes. Also, there were fourteen colored panes in each of the stained glass windows. I should have done this the day we moved in, she thought when she discovered that the window seat in the front hallway concealed a perfect hiding place. But she found no glasses. She found nothing but the same pieces of furniture she had been living with for eleven years and stacks of cardboard boxes filled with stuff that nobody had needed enough to un-pack yet.

I will not accept defeat, she told herself sternly. Up the stairs she went to search the second floor. In the room that Nell and Nora shared she found nothing; in her father's tiny office, nothing; in her parents' bedroom, nothing. Miri cautiously opened the door to Ray and Robbie's room. It wasn't offi-cially off-limits, but the door was usually closed. She tried to remember if they had ever invited her to come and hang out with them in their room. She didn't think so. Not that it was such a lovely place to hang out, Miri thought, looking around. Robbie and Ray had not wasted much time unpacking. Their posters drooped, unrolling, in corners, and their books were still stacked next to the bookcase.

On Ray's side of the room, clothes were scattered on the floor like fallen plums. Robbie's side was neater. He had even decorated a little: his A+ ziggurat diagram hung over his bed, side by side with a small, blurry photograph of their cat, Icky, who had died two summers ago. Miri squinted, trying to see beyond all the familiar junk. It was impossible. She glanced from the half pickle floating in a jar to a brownish tank that (in theory) held a couple of lizards to a gutted Walkman lying on a piece of newspaper. There was a lot of stuff. But there was nothing that would contain seventy-year-old glasses. Miri was turning to go when her eyes fell on the closet.

The closet had no door. It *had* had a door, but the door was now leaning against the wall next to Ray's bed. So Miri could see inside the closet. And what she saw, rising above the smelly rubble of shoes and shirts, was a ladder built against the back wall of the closet. It led up to a small door, set high in the wall.

The attic.

Of course. Miri had known, even before her adventure with Molly, that there was an attic, because her own room was right next to it. And she knew that the nailed-down flap in her own closet could not be the only way into it, because that would be stupid. But she hadn't thought much about it. Now she did. The attic would obviously be the place for Flo, Horst, Sissy, and—Miri crossed her fingers—Molly to store old stuff and forget about it. She remembered the napping dressmaker's dummy. There should be tons of stuff up there by now. She jumped through the mess on the closet floor and took hold of the ladder's rungs.

At the top, the door opened with a squeak of protest, and Miri rapidly hoisted herself in, scraping her knees as she went. The attic was hot and dusty, just as it had been over seventy years before, and the same thin slats of light angled across the floor from the air vent. The first thing Miri saw as she climbed through the door were three pillows lined up on the floor, and her stomach jumped with illogical hope— Molly! She whirled around, ready to find her friend.

Nothing.

Beyond the pillows, the attic was empty. The floor that stretched away into dark corners was bare. It contained not one thing that Molly had ever touched. Hot tears filled Miri's eyes and her throat grew thick. What if I never find her? she thought with an ache. What if I never know what happened? Two bright drops shimmered on the dusty floor, and she smeared them away. "Molly," she called in a low voice. "C'mere." She knew that there would be no answer, but she waited anyway. Nothing. "I'm not going to quit," she said into the silent attic. She didn't sound very convincing. "I'm *not* going to quit." That was better.

Miri climbed down the ladder, too gloomy even to plug her nose against the socky stink. She thumped heavily down the stairs and out the back door. Her mother was weeding the little vegetable patch near the porch while Nell and Nora squabbled over the tire swing nearby.

Miri glared at the neat rows of tomato plants. "Rhododendrons would look better," she snapped.

"You can't eat rhododendrons." Her mother didn't even look up from her work.

Humph, thought Miri. She should be nicer to me if she doesn't want me to run away again. The thought made her smile—she was starting to believe that running-away story herself.

Her mother smiled in return. "That's better. Do you want to go to town now?"

"For new glasses?"

"And paint, too."

"Mom?"

"Hmm?"

"Could I get wallpaper instead?"

Her mother made a face. "You want wallpaper? What kind?"

"I saw one with pink roses. I thought it was pretty." Miri tried to keep her face blank.

"Pink roses?" Her mother stared at her. "That sounds kind of old-fashioned."

"Remember? I like old-fashioned stuff," said Miri.

"Well. Okay, honey. It might be kind of a stretch for Paxton Hardware, but we'll see if they have any wallpaper with pink roses." Miri could see that her mother was trying to be positive. She smiled a secret smile. This guilt thing was great.

"Let's go, then," she said.

·: CHAPTER :·

10

"THESE ARE CUTE," said her mother, holding up a pair of emerald green frames.

Miri didn't think anyone wore emerald green glasses in 1935. She didn't want to stand out too much. "No thanks. I think I want these." She selected a pair of brown tortoiseshell glasses.

"You're sure?" her mother said. "They're a little plain, aren't they?"

"They're fine." Miri turned to the red-faced man behind the counter. "When can they be ready?"

"You name it," he said and winked at her.

"Today?"

"Today? We're fast, but we're not that fast, little lady." He chuckled, as though she was being childish.

Miri decided she didn't like him. "I thought Speedi-Spec meant you could do them in a day," she said in her most adult voice.

His face got redder. "A day means twenty-four hours. We'll have them ready tomorrow."

"What time?" she persisted.

He scowled at her. "Noon."

"That will be great," her mother interrupted, shooting Miri a look that said Stop Being a Pest.

I'm not being a pest, Miri thought back. I'm just standing up for myself. And Molly.

Miri and her mother walked up the street to Paxton Hardware. Waves of heat jiggled off the sidewalk, and Miri wiped the back of her neck with her hand. It was a lot cooler at home than it was in town.

"Where did those boys go?" her mother muttered, and her question was answered almost instantly, for Robbie and Ray appeared looking aggravated, with Nell and Nora trailing behind, happily eating long, sticky strands of red licorice.

"Sorry, Mom, but they wouldn't stop whining," Ray answered his mother's outraged face.

"Boys! You know they're not supposed to have candy!"

"It's good, Mama!" said Nora enthusiastically. "You want some?"

"Yeah," said Robbie, yanking the entire string of licorice out of her hands. "Here, Mom." He handed it to his mother proudly, as though he had solved the problem.

Nora began to cry, and Nell, sensing trouble, quickly balled up her licorice and jammed the whole thing in her mouth. While her mother soothed Nora and persuaded Nell to spit the giant wad out, Miri leaned against a hot fire hydrant. No telling how long it would take to stop the crying.

She looked at the bright Astroturf in front of the fast-food place. Now that was totally weird. She imagined trying to explain Astroturf to Molly—it's fake grass that doesn't look like grass, and every-body knows it's fake, but they put it on the ground and everyone pretends it's real. Miri smiled, think-ing of Molly's face. Next to the fast-food place was Maydale's Health and Nutrition One-Stop Shop, which smelled like pills. Next door to that was Bead-Quest. Miri liked that store; she liked the sound the beads made in their little boxes when she stirred them with her finger. She didn't think they had bead shops in 1935. Molly would like BeadQuest.

She glanced behind her. Now Nell was crying. A tiny, bent man was hobbling across the street, bringing the slow traffic of Paxton to a halt. He didn't seem to notice. Or maybe he was just so old he didn't care. Now the curb was giving him trouble; Miri watched as he wiped his hands on his trousers and gripped his cane tightly. Slowly, slowly, he lifted one foot to the curb, and, bracing himself with the cane, hoisted the rest of his tiny body up. Miri was fascinated. He must be a hundred years old. He shuffled past her, across the sidewalk to a dingy storefront.

A crooked screen door squealed as he pulled it open and entered. What kind of store was it, she wondered, banging her feet against the fire hydrant. There were shelves in the window, but there wasn't much on them. A few old teacups and a fish stuck on a piece of wood. Miri squinted at the chipped gold lettering on the dirty window: U AND I TRADING POST, it said, and down below: R. GUEST, PROP. Miri couldn't imagine anyone wanting that fish, no matter what. The U and I Trading Post had probably been around for a hundred years, easy.

A hundred years.

What about seventy years? Miri stopped kicking the hydrant.

R. Guest, Prop.

Guest.

Wait.

She remembered: "He's this old guy, like really old, who's lived in the valley for like a million years." Mr. Guest had told Robbie and Ray about the stolen stuff.

Miri stood up. That old man was Mr. Guest himself. She knew it. And she had to talk to him. He had probably known them: Horst, Flo, and Sissy. And maybe even—hope blazed up again like fire—Molly.

"Where are you going?" It was her mother's voice. "Let's get along to the hardware store and see about that wallpaper. Boys, I'm counting on you this time." She turned to Miri.

And Miri, who could come up with no reasonable explanation for an urgent trip to the U and I Trading Post, trailed dismally after her mother in the direction of Paxton Hardware.

. . .

Twenty minutes later, Miri scuttled out of the hardware store like an escaped prisoner, looking over her shoulder. The pink rose wallpaper had been chosen, and as her mother began a long and boring conversation with the clerk about wallpaper paste, Miri quickly whispered, "Can I go to the library?"

Her mother nodded absently. "How long does it take to dry?" she said to the clerk.

Miri hurried down the street to the U and I Trading Post. She yanked open the dirty screen door and whisked in, her heart thumping.

Inside, the shop was silent, the cool air heavy with oldness. The shelves inside the store didn't contain much more than the ones in the window—a few old trays and lampshades and things like that.

"Looking for something, missy?" quavered an ancient voice.

Miri couldn't see him at first, because he was as old and dingy as the wall behind him. Mr. Guest was sitting on a stool behind a splintery counter, peering at a newspaper. He looked like a statue, Miri thought, like one of those weird gnomes people stick in their front yards.

"Actually, um, I'm . . . well, I'm looking—for you," she blurted, her face hot.

He didn't seem surprised. "That right, missy?" He laid down his newspaper with care.

"Yes. I need to ask you about some people who used to live here—well, not here exactly, but out on Pickering Lane."

He nodded, his eyes bright. "Yes'm. You kin to those hooligans just moved out there?"

Miri giggled. "You mean those boys you met yesterday? They're my brothers."

Mr. Guest's teeth were abnormally large and white. "Thought so. They don't know much about fishing."

Miri took a breath. "Mr. Guest, did you know Flo and—and Sissy and—and Horst?" Her voice trailed off; she couldn't bring herself to say Molly's name. "I don't know their last name, but they lived in my house about seventy years ago."

Mr. Guest responded with a wheezing sound that Miri hoped was a laugh. "Sure I knew Flo and Sissy. Still do. Sissy, leastways."

"She's alive?" gasped Miri. She had never thought of that.

"You could say so. Her kids moved her on out to O-hi-o," he drew the word out like it was some sort of strange contraption. "Her girl has a place up at Marion, O-hi-o. They figured Sis was too old to take care of herself, even though she's a spring chicken compared to me. I'm ninety-four last May." He wheezed with pride.

Miri could tell she was supposed to say something about that. "Wow," she replied, trying to sound enthusiastic. "That's old."

"Yessiree. Poor Sis was getting a little creaky, all by her lonesome in that big house."

Miri couldn't contain herself any longer. "Did you know a girl who lived there in 1935? Eleven years old? Her name is Molly Gardner. Do you know anything about her?"

Now the old man peered at her. "'35? Who said anything about '35? I didn't get here till '37. I was twenty-five years old in '37, and I bought my first sixty acres out there by the Woodmill place."

Miri didn't want to hear about acres. She wanted to hear about Molly. "But did you ever hear of a girl? When you came here in '37?"

"A girl? Out to Bains's? Can't say I did. There weren't any little girls out there in '37, far as I know."

"Oh," said Miri, shoulders slumping.

"All I heard was about Horst. Heard plenty about him."

Miri swallowed. She didn't know how to ask what she wanted to know. And she wasn't sure she wanted to know it. "What did you hear about Horst?"

"That he was a thief," said Mr. Guest bluntly. "That he stole everything that wasn't nailed down, but just little things. Little jewelry from the local ladies. Little bit from the shops. Little cash from the till. Storekeepers hated to see him coming. That's mostly what you heard about Horst—that he was a thief." Mr. Guest sniffled a long sniffle. "But some said he was worse'n that." He nodded solemnly.

Miri's throat shriveled. "Worse how?" she croaked.

Mr. Guest bent toward her confidentially. "Effie Fletcher, she was school principal here for more'n forty years—she said a meaner fellow than Horst Bains never drew breath."

Miri felt herself relax. No big deal. A school principal wasn't very likely to think Horst was a great guy.

But Mr. Guest wasn't finished. "And Effie Fletcher always vowed that Horst Bains was a killer."

"No!" Miri shouted and then clapped her hand over her mouth.

Mr. Guest looked offended. "All right, all right. I ain't saying it's true." He drew a handkerchief from his pocket and patted his neck with it. "I'm just telling you what Effie sa—"

"Why?" interrupted Miri. "Excuse me, but *why* did she think that—that—he—" she stuttered, unable to continue.

"Hah," said Mr. Guest, folding his handkerchief thoughtfully. "Can't say I know *why*. Just Effie spreading tales, I expect. Used to send Sissy into a tailspin when she'd hear about Effie vowing her brother was a killer. She'd say Horst wasn't perfect but he never killed anyone." Mr. Guest's white teeth glinted in a smile. "She had a real high voice when she got mad, Sissy did."

"What about Horst?" asked Miri. "What did he say?"

Mr. Guest's bright eyes rested on her curiously. "Horst? Why, he was long gone by then."

"Gone? You never met him?"

The old man shook his head. "Naw. He lit out before I got here."

"Lit out? What do you mean?"

"Ran away. Adelie Kent always said that he found out the sheriff was on his tail, and he took off. He stole something or other from her, and she was mad about it until the day she died."

"Her pink gold bracelet," remembered Miri.

For the first time, Mr. Guest looked startled. "How'd you know that?"

Caught. "Um," Miri bumbled. "I heard it somewhere."

"You ain't found that old stuff, have you?" he asked in a sharp voice.

"No. No," Miri said. "I haven't found anything. And anyway, why wouldn't he have taken it when he ran away? You'd think he would."

"Well, but there's the story." The old man nodded knowingly. "They used to tell it, how the day he run off—couple years before I got here—he come into Pickus Drugstore middle of one summer afternoon, his face white as a sheet. 'I got to get outta here,' he says to Dusty Burdet behind the soda counter, 'and you got to give me some cash.' Dusty says no, which took some guts, because Horst is twice the size of anybody, and then Horst leans over the counter and grabs him by the collar. Dusty always said Horst was sweating like a pig, with big drops running off his chin. And Horst says, 'Gimme twenty-five dollars and put it on my mama's account afore I kill you.'"

Miri leaned forward, mesmerized. "And did he?"

Mr. Guest leaned forward, too. "You bet he did. On the double. And that's the last anyone saw of Horst Bains."

"The last?" squeaked Miri. Running away didn't sound like Horst—it took courage.

Mr. Guest nodded.

"But—but why?" she asked. "Why'd he run away?"

He shrugged. "No one knows. And no one ever found any stolen jewelry, either, so maybe he didn't steal it atall. Folks like to gossip. Dusty said he looked like he'd seen a ghost."

"A ghost," murmured Miri. She sat quiet for a moment, thinking. "When did you say this happened?" she asked suddenly.

"Couple years before I came. Maybe '35."

"1935?" Miri gulped. "And it was a summer afternoon? That's what you said, right?"

"Kids are sharp these days," said Mr. Guest. "Adelie Kent always said it was a summer day. Who knows? Adelie's been dead for about thirty years."

Miri stared at Mr. Guest's cash register without seeing it. Why would Horst run away? "A ghost," she said. Horst would run away if he was too scared to stay at home. "Maybe he did see a ghost." Her brain circled the idea she didn't want to have, but there was no avoiding it, not anymore. Horst would run away if he had killed Molly and thought he was going to get caught. Effie Fletcher, who always vowed Horst was a killer, was the school principal—someone who would have known Molly—someone who would have noticed when she didn't return to school in September. I've got to get back, I've got to get back and stop him, Miri thought wretchedly, gnawing at her knuckle. What if he kills her? He's mean enough. He hates her enough. He wouldn't. He might. *Got to get back.*

"Whatsa matter, missy?" asked Mr. Guest. "You look a little ghosty yourself."

"Oh, I'm okay." Miri took a step backward and stopped. "Say, Mr. Guest, you don't have any old glasses in your store, do you?"

"Glasses. Sure. Got a couple over there." He waved his arm at a shelf holding four yellow drinking glasses.

"No. Eyeglasses. Old eyeglasses," said Miri.

Mr. Guest's face wrinkled up like a walnut. "Eyeglasses? What for? You can't use other folks' glasses. Such a thing as prescriptions, you know."

"Not to use. I collect them," lied Miri.

"Huh. Never heard of such a thing. I don't carry old specs," he said disapprovingly.

"Okay. That's okay. Well, thanks, Mr. Guest. You've really helped me out. Thanks a lot." She waved as she moved toward the door.

He watched her, saying nothing until her hand was on the screen door. "Let me know if you find that jewelry, missy," he said, before turning back to his newspaper.

·: CHAPTER :·

11

ON THE RIDE HOME, as her brothers and sisters gabbled around her, Miri was quiet. *Got to get back to Molly. Got to get back to Molly.* It was like a song she couldn't get out of her head. *Got to get back before . . .*

"I'm sorry you've been a bad girl all day and you have to go to bed with your stomach hungry to teach you a lesson." Nell's voice interrupted her thoughts. "You're time-out," she announced to her doll.

"What'd she do this time?" asked Robbie, leaning over the back of her seat. He was bored.

"She spilled her milk," Nell said sternly. "She's a bad girl."

"That's not fair. You spill milk all the time," Robbie argued. "And you don't get a time-out for it."

"Mama, Robbie's being mean to me," began Nell.

"I'm from the Society for the Prevention of Cruelty to Dolls," he said. "You're a rotten mom."

Miri patted her sister's fat hand. "Don't pay any attention to him. He's just bugging you because he hasn't got anything else to do."

Robbie made a sound like a siren. "Once again, the SPCD arrives in the nick of time, saving this poor child from her cruel mother."

"Another child rescued from a life of misery," added Ray. Reaching around Nell's booster seat, he plucked the doll from her arms and began to sing, "Rock-a-bye, baby, on the tree— Oh no!" He shook the doll in his hands. "She's trying to jump! I can't hold her back! Ahh!" He pretended to fumble with it, and—so quick Nell couldn't see—he tucked the doll behind his back. "Oh no!" he gasped. "She jumped out the window. Nell! Your baby's in the middle of the road! She's dead!"

"Ray!" called their mother. "You didn't!"

Nell began to wail. "My Sierra!"

"I didn't do it, Mom," protested Ray. "She jumped to her death. I tried to stop her."

Robbie joined in, chortling, "She had to get away from her cruel mother."

"She didn't! She loves me!" howled Nell, with Nora joining in.

"Well, you can go right back and get it," announced their mother, slowing the car. "And then you can walk home."

"Aw, Mom, we're just joshing." Ray pulled the doll from behind his back and tossed it into the seat in front of him, where Nell fell on it with screams and kisses.

"You guys are meanies," said Miri. She hugged the top of Nell's head.

"And you can still walk home," said their mother, pulling to a stop by the side of the road. "Out. That was a rotten trick, and I won't allow that kind of unkindness in my car. Out."

"Mom!" moaned Ray. "We didn't throw the doll out. We were just kidding!"

"It was mean, and I won't have it." All of her children recognized the Don't Mess With Me voice.

"Nell's meaner than we are," grumbled Robbie. "A time-out for spilling milk. That's crazy."

"Out."

"Mom! It's sweltering!" pleaded Ray.

"Out."

Silently, the boys climbed out of the car and stood on the side of the road with pathetic faces. As their mother pulled away from the roadside, Miri, Nell, and Nora turned for one final look from the back window. "Mom, they're hitchhiking," said Miri.

Mom did not seem concerned. "Ha. They wouldn't dare. And besides—nobody uses this road. They'll walk."

"They're bad," announced Nora. "They stole."

"They lied, too," said Miri.

"They stole and they lied," said Nell.

Like Horst, thought Miri. But he stole and lied for real. He wasn't fooling around like Ray and Robbie were. He didn't joke, even when he was joking. She remembered his thick voice saying, "You reckon old Molly's got an allergic to glass? Din't she lose her specs just last week? Seems like glass and her just don't get along." That almost sounded like something Ray and Robbie would say, but it was a lot meaner coming from Horst. You could tell he just loved getting Molly in trouble. He probably took her glasses himself, Miri thought. Just to get her in trouble. He probably hid them—

"Oh my God!" she said out loud.

"What?" said her mother, braking again.

"Nothing!" said Miri quickly. "Sorry. I just thought of something. Nothing." That was it! She would bet anything in the world that Horst had taken Molly's glasses and hidden them in the barn. She remembered the glinting light she had spied from the loft. She had thought then that it was jewelry, but it could have been glass. It could have been Molly's glasses! All she had to do was dig them up.

Miri began to whack her feet against the floor of the car. "This is taking forever," she said.

"Stop that," said her mother. "We're almost home."

Almost home. Almost.

The tires crunched onto gravel.

Finally.

. . .

The smooth handle of the shovel slipped against her sweating hands as Miri lifted the weight of it up and slammed it down with all her strength.

There was a moist, splintery sound as it plunged into something under the surface of the earth and stuck fast, and Miri let out a breath she hadn't even known she was holding. She knelt to scratch away the dirt, and her heart began to gallop wildly, because she saw that the shovel had cut into a rotten board just below the soil. It was an old piece of barn floor, the wood nearly decayed—all she needed to do was shove up the edge over there, and pull it away from the chunk of gray brick that held it in place. Once more, she turned to look up at the spot where she thought the loft had been. If she had remembered the shape of the barn right, this was *almost* sure to be the place she had seen Horst digging.

She burrowed her fingers into the earth until she found the bottom edge of the board, and then she yanked upward. The slimy wood slipped out of her hands and back into place. Miri took a deep breath, dug her fingers under the edge of the wood again, and heaved upward. This time it came. With a squealing creak, the board pulled away from the gray brick and toppled over.

Underneath was a hole. It wasn't a big hole, and weeds and spiderwebs and slug-things filled most of it, but there in the middle was a metal chest the size of a shoe box.

Miri sat back on her heels. It was Horst's box. She had found it. She stared at the box, her breath coming in little pants. She had found it.

The glasses. Were they inside?

She couldn't stand to look.

She couldn't stand not to look.

Miri forced herself to reach into the hole and lift out the box. Then she paused for a moment, gathering courage. The black metal was rusted through in some places, and its clasp hung uselessly by a single nail. There was no lock. Slowly, she stretched out her hand and opened the lid. A wet, rotting smell rose up, and the first thing she saw were several large, bug-eaten brown lumps that had probably once been paper. Then the glint of metal caught her eye, and, poking the lumps to one side, she found a little collection of jewelry. Horst's loot. There was a tarnished watch, the kind you wear on a chain; a ring with dark red stones; two gold lockets; a cameo pin; and a gold bracelet.

"The pink gold bracelet," she whispered, though it didn't look especially pink.

But where were the glasses? Miri prodded the brown lumps again and then pulled them out, looking for the shine of glass. They had to be here. They *had* to be here. With the first sharp prick of desperation, she picked up the box and shook it.

Something rattled.

There was another bottom. Miri yanked at the top tray and it gave way, breaking into pieces in her hands. And, underneath, was Horst's most secret secret: a small rectangular metal box. Miri snatched at the box and wrenched it open. There, lying calmly on a piece of yellowed cloth, was a pair of eyeglasses. One of its thin metal rims held nothing, but the other encircled a fragile lens. Just one. But one was all she needed. "Oh boy," Miri whispered. "Oh boy oh boy oh boy." With exquisite caution, she turned the delicate frames over. The lens was clear and unbroken. It was perfect. It even looked magic. Okay, not really. But she knew it would work. She had found her ticket to Molly, and all she had to do was keep it safe. She placed the glasses back in the case and hugged it to her. "Okay," she assured herself. "Okay, okay, okay. I'm almost there."

Her thoughts were running around like hamsters,

and she tried to collect them. What's next? Okay. Next, I have to get my new glasses so we can come back. Tomorrow at noon. Noon. Okay. She tried to breathe calmly. "I'll be there as soon as I can, Molly." *I hope that's soon enough,* said the voice in her head. She chewed on her knuckles, thinking. Molly either hadn't found or hadn't taken Horst's stash. Maybe that means she didn't run away. *Maybe that means he killed her,* the voice whispered. Shut *up,* she told it.

"On your mark! Get set!" It was Ray, bellowing from the end of the driveway. *"Go!"*

Quickly, Miri shoved the glasses case down her shirt. Scrabbling the brown lumps back into the box, she plucked out the bracelet and put it in her pocket. She would give that to Mr. Guest to return to Adelie Kent's family.

"No way! You cheated!" Ray was hollering as Robbie bolted into the backyard. "You totally cheated!"

Miri turned to watch Robbie run a victory lap around Ray.

"You were already running when you said 'Go,'" argued Ray. "I *saw* you." He threw himself down on the lawn. "I got heatstroke."

Now Robbie noticed her. "Whatcha doing, Miri?"

Miri looked at him, thinking. Should she hide the box, keep it a secret? Should she make up a lie, fight to keep it hers alone?

Why? What was the point?

She had Molly and magic. She didn't need to have the treasure, too. Finding it was the good part anyway. She had the special—her brothers could have the extra.

Robbie made a farting noise. "What are you— catatonic? Wake up!"

"It's the stolen stuff," she said quietly. "I found it."

Ray sat up like he'd been jerked on a string. "What?"

The boys scrambled across the lawn, bumping into each other as they knelt beside her. "Where?"

"Here. It was under this board." Miri pointed to the rotting plank.

Together, her brothers' wide eyes moved from the battered metal box to the weed-choked hole. Ray whistled softly. "Wow."

"Mir," said Robbie, "How'd you know—?"

"It was here?" Ray looked at her with awe.

Miri couldn't resist torturing them. "I just had a feeling," she said mysteriously. "I was sitting in the car this afternoon, and all of a sudden, I had a vision of where it was."

"Aw, come on, don't give us that," began Ray, but Robbie hit him on the arm.

"Shut up. Don't argue with her." He turned to his sister respectfully. "Can we open it? Huh?"

"Sure," said Miri, enjoying her power. She didn't tell them she had already opened it.

Robbie reached out, but Ray was quicker. He yanked the lid off unceremoniously. The familiar rotting smell wafted up as they stared into the mess of brown lumps. "What's this? Looks like dog turds," he said, poking them with his finger. "But hey—check it out—jewelry!" Ray pulled out the watch and then the other pieces, and laid them reverently on the grass.

"Whoa," Robbie said quietly. For a long moment, the two boys stared in silence.

Then Ray said, "How much you think we can get for them?"

"They're antiques," said Robbie. "People pay a lot for antiques."

"Thousands?"

"Maybe," said Robbie. "Hey look, a ring!" He picked up the ring. "It's gold."

"Got to be worth something." Ray sounded like he had a college degree in jewelry.

Miri watched as Robbie inspected one of the wads of brown paper. "Ray," he said, slowly peeling the mess apart. "Dude."

"Huh?" Ray was prying open one of the lockets.

"It isn't dog turds. It's money!"

Miri leaned over. In the middle of the wad, you could see that the paper had markings on it. It did look like dollar bills. And it made sense that Horst would keep money in his secret hiding place.

Ray dropped the locket and picked up a brown lump. "Money," he said softly. "Think we can spend it?"

Robbie fingered the lump. "Maybe. Maybe if we dry it out. Or maybe we can sell it to people who collect old money."

Ray grinned. "Yeah! It's probably worth even more that way! We can get an iPod!"

"Or an Xbox," said Robbie dreamily. "Or both."

"Sure. We're rich!" Ray rubbed his hands together and cackled gleefully, like a cartoon villain. "Rich, rich, rich."

Robbie stopped. He looked at Miri, his round blue eyes thoughtful. "But it's yours, really," he said.

"What?" Ray stared at him in astonishment. "You're crazy! It's not hers!"

"She found it," Robbie said stubbornly. "Finders keepers. That's fair."

Robbie always worried about fair. Miri suddenly remembered the time the police officer visiting her first-grade classroom had run out of traffic-safety coloring books right when he came to her. Robbie had been so outraged he had drawn a special traffic-safety coloring book, just for her. She still had it. She smiled at him. "I don't really care about the stuff," she said, thinking of the glasses tucked in her shirt. "I just wanted to find it."

He wasn't convinced. "Yeah, and you did. So you should at least take something. Take the pin."

"Yeah," agreed Ray, nodding eagerly. "The pin's pretty." He held it out to her. "See, it's got a girl on it. You can have it. We'd probably have enough for the iPod without it."

"No. I don't want the pin," Miri said. "But guys. Don't you think you should find out who it belonged to? Maybe they're still alive."

They looked at her resentfully. "No way," said Ray, after a moment. "This stuff has been here for almost a hundred years. Whoever it belonged to is dead for sure."

Robbie nodded. "Got to be." But he didn't sound quite so certain.

"What if it's only been, like, seventy years," Miri argued. "The owners might still be alive."

"Nah, it takes at least a hundred years for metal to rust out like that. We did oxidation in science last year," said Ray. Now he sounded like he had a college degree in rust.

Miri puffed her cheeks full of air and let it out slowly. There was nothing she could say, nothing that would not reveal her secret journey to Molly's world. "Well," she said finally, "I found it, so I have some say in what happens to it. And I say you should ask Mr. Guest."

"Huh? Mr. Guest? That old guy? Why?" said Robbie.

"'Cause he might know who the stuff belongs to," said Miri.

They stared at her, obviously wondering why she cared more about strangers than about them getting rich. Robbie's eyes narrowed. "Mir," he began, "really. How did you figure out where it was?"

Uh-oh. Time to go. "I'm a witch," said Miri. She rolled her eyes around.

"You're a loon," said Ray. He turned to his brother. "Do you think Mom would really let us get an Xbox?"

Miri stood up, and the glasses rattled down to the waistband of her shorts. Her hand in her pocket touched the thin strands of the pink gold bracelet. She had what she needed. It wasn't going to be long now.

Hope it's not too late, said her brain. *Shut up,* she said again, walking across the lawn.

~: **CHAPTER** :~

12

HORST BROUGHT HIS FACE close to hers. Thin streams of sweat leaked down from his oiled hair, and his flabby cheeks were grayish pink. Miri took a step back. She didn't want his sweat to get on her glasses and wreck them. But he caught her T-shirt up in his fist and pulled her toward him. His slab-lips opened and he growled, "Who said you could take my stuff? Who?"

Miri woke with a jump. Horrible! Her heart was thumping, and she peered anxiously into her dark room. Was he hiding in the shadows? Slowly, her mind limped back to the real world: it was just a dream. Horst had been dead for years. She hoped.

She shivered and turned on the lamp next to her

bed. What time was it? She couldn't see across the room to her clock, so she padded to her desk. 4:45. The sun would rise soon. What a relief. She had been waking up all night long, chased by Horst from one dream to another. She shook her head, trying to dislodge the memory. Horst was worse than any nightmare monster in the world. Well, almost. Two Halloweens ago, Ray had a zombie mask that had completely freaked her out. She dreamed about that thing every night for a month. Okay—Horst was a close second then, with his streams of sweat and grayish skin.

Climbing back into bed, Miri gave up on sleep. She propped herself up on her pillows and looked at the corner of the room where she had found the glass lens. What if I hadn't found it? she wondered. Or was it my destiny—I *had* to find it on that particular day? Miri, girl of destiny. Yeah, right. How could it be my destiny? I only saw the glass when I was sent to my room. And I was only sent to my room because I hit Ray. And I only hit Ray because he tripped me. What if none of those things had happened?

She wedged the pillows under her head and

thought. Maybe there isn't one thing that *has* to happen. Maybe there are a bunch of different possibilities for every minute. Miri closed her eyes and tried to picture it. Maybe time is like being in a hallway with four doors; if you open the one on the right, you'll end up in another hall with four more doors. But if you chose the door on the left, you'd end up somewhere else entirely. So what happens changes all the time, depending on what people choose. Miri pulled her sheets up to her neck as a breeze curled through the little room.

But all the 1935 stuff has already happened, so I can't change it, because it's in the past.

But maybe the past can change, too, the voice in her brain countered. *Think of the frying pan chipping the floor. It became the past.*

But if the past changes, wouldn't that make everything different in the present? Miri wondered.

Maybe it is different, and we don't even know it.

Her eyes clicked open. That was a weird idea. That would mean that the past didn't have to turn out the way she thought it did.

It could turn out better.

Or worse.

Okay, so what happened in the past changes because I went there, like when I dropped the frying pan. But what if it changes so that Molly's lens isn't in my room two days ago? What then?

Then it will be erased. From inside me, too. I won't know anything about Molly because it will not have happened.

Not knowing about Molly? That would be the worst of all.

It's *got* to happen.

Everything's got to turn out just the way it has. Unless Horst has—

Grimly, Miri began to chew on her knuckle. She didn't want to think it. But she had to. I can't change it if he's already killed her, she thought. But let's say—let's say he hasn't done anything—yet. Then I can change history. I'll change it by bringing Molly home.

Her knuckle hurt from all the chewing it had had lately. Miri took an experimental bite of her thumbnail. Not so good, but better than nothing.

Okay. But what about Horst? If he ran away because he—Miri took a breath—did something bad to Molly, then he wouldn't run away if she kept him from doing it. And if he didn't run away, he might just take the glasses out of his buried box some time between 1935 and now. And then it wouldn't be there for her to find yesterday. And then she wouldn't be able to go get Molly. She couldn't allow that. No matter what, she had to have the lens so she could go back to get Molly. And what about the lens that was on her wall in the first place? She had to make sure that one was put up, too. Right now, it was somewhere in Molly's room. She hoped.

Okay. Fine. When she went back to 1935 to get Molly, she'd put one lens up on the wall, put the other one back under the barn floor, and then she'd make Horst run away.

How the heck was she going to do all that?

Getting the lenses in the right places—that didn't seem too hard. But getting rid of Horst? Impossible.

The first businesslike call of a bird sounded outside. It was nearly day. She was glad to leave night and dreams behind. She hoped Horst wouldn't hang around in her dreams for weeks the way the zombie had.

Hey. Wait.

In Miri's mind, a tiny idea began to flicker to life.

He looked like he'd seen a ghost, Mr. Guest had said. Sweating like a pig. Scared half to death.

Miri sat up straight. It wouldn't be a ghost that scared him, because she was going to make sure that Molly didn't become a ghost. But maybe she could make Horst scared enough to run away anyway.

The idea grew bigger, and Miri smiled. It could even be fun.

. . .

"What time is it?"

"It's ten minutes after the last time you asked me," her mother replied. "What's the matter with you?"

"I want my glasses."

"They're not ready yet."

. . .

"Mom, when are we going to *go*?"

"Stop pestering me. We'll go soon."

"How soon is soon?"

"An hour. Stop pestering me."

"An *hour*? Please, can we go before that? I'll wash the dishes for a week."

"Why are you so crazy to get your glasses?"

"Because I am. Please, Mom. Please, please, please."

• • •

"How many more miles?"

"Not another word, Miri."

"I thought we had to be nice to Miri, Mama," piped up Nell.

"I *am* being nice. I'm taking her into town even though it's not convenient for me to go right now. That's nice."

"I love you, Mom."

"Right. Butter me up."

• • •

"That'll be $114.62, Mrs. Gill."

"Lord. Miri, you may not break these."

Miri nodded. Sure, Mom.

"Thank you kindly, Mrs. Gill. You all have a nice day."

"Thank you."

"Let's go home."

"Miri! Can you say thank you to Mr. Deetz?"

"Thanks, Mr. Deetz. The glasses are very nice. Let's go home."

. . .

"Okay. First thing is lunch. Miri, will you make a couple of PB and Js for the girls? I'll make quesadillas for you and the guys."

"Mom, I really have to do something right now. I don't need any lunch—"

"Not so fast, sister. I drove you into town because you *had* to get your glasses. Seems only fair that you help me with lunch. This house is not a restaurant, you know, and I am not—"

"Okay, okay, okay. Jeez . . ."

"Stop sighing."

. . .

Miri tossed the last cup into the dishwasher. She wished she hadn't said that bit about washing the dishes for a week. At least it was over now. She ignored the crumbs and spilled milk on the counter and ran up the stairs to her brothers' room.

Robbie and Ray were conveniently outside, excavating the barn in search of further loot. The wads of rotting money had been set out carefully to dry on the top of Robbie's dresser, but Miri didn't stop to inspect. She had to hurry. Every moment could be the one she was dreading, the one she had to stop from happening. Quickly, she made her way to the closet. She had to dig through layers of magazines, computer paper, folders, shoes, socks, ripped T-shirts, and skateboards before she finally found the lopsided canvas sack that contained old Halloween costumes. She yanked out a Darth Whatever mask and a big pink bag from the year Robbie had been an eraser and threw them on the floor. Where was the stupid thing? This was taking too long. She turned the bag upside down and shook it until costumes rained down—and then she jumped, because there it was, grinning up at her. Ray's zombie mask. It still gave her the creeps. Miri forced herself to reach out and pick it up. Yuck. She tucked it into her shirt, shivering as it touched her skin, and was just turning to go when she stopped. The CD player. She opened the top and saw that the Deathbag CD was still in the machine. Sound effects. She picked up the player and ran out of the room.

. . .

Miri froze in the doorway of her bedroom.

"Oh, good. I could use some help." Her mother was at the top of a ladder, peeling the purple wallpaper off the wall in long strips. "You can start over there, near the floor."

Miri opened her mouth, and a choked sound came out.

"What's the matter? It's actually kind of fun—I feel like I'm doing something against the rules, pulling paper off the walls."

"Mom?" Miri's voice was tight. "I have to return this CD player to Ray. Right away."

Her mother turned around. "What's the matter with your throat?"

But Miri was already gone.

.   .   .

Miri felt like screaming. Now Ray was in his room, using the hair dryer on the brown wads. Nell and Nora's room had Nell and Nora in it. Robbie was in her parents' bedroom, checking the cost of Play-Stations on her father's computer.

Fuming, Miri thundered down the stairs. She had pictured returning in her room—Molly's room—but her mom was ruining everything. Fine, then, I'll use her office, thought Miri. It doesn't matter. Nothing matters except getting there. She stepped quickly through the dark hall at the bottom of the stairs and into her mother's box-crowded office. I hope this room was here in 1935, she thought, looking at the array of windows along one wall. The glass was bubbly and old looking, but she didn't know for sure. She might end up in the rhododendrons again. Doesn't matter, she repeated. Nothing matters except getting there. A cool breeze played along her shoulder blades, though the afternoon heat was heavy and still outside the windows.

Cautiously, she pulled Molly's glasses case out of her pocket and opened it. The single lens glinted weakly inside its metal frame. They looked like joke glasses, ridiculous glasses. Not at all important. Not at all magical. *Oh, let this work,* she pleaded. *Please.*

Gently, Miri opened the thin arm pieces and readied her stomach for the lunge into time. Okay, she reminded herself. One lens on the wall. One lens in the barn. One big, mean, possible murderer chased away. No problem. Miri took a breath and patted the bulk of Ray's mask, which was stuffed tightly into her waistband.

Let me go back, she thought.

Miri grasped the CD player in one hand and

slipped on Molly's glasses with the other. She had everything she needed. She was ready to go back. She blinked away the tears that came immediately, half from excitement, half from the lens. The books that lined the office walls dipped and wavered and then seemed to melt away, surging up as she sank sickeningly down.

☽ CHAPTER ☾

13

MIRI LAY FLAT on her back on a polished wood floor. Directly above her, about three inches from the end of her nose, was a mattress. She closed her eyes and opened them again. The mattress was still there. She was under a bed. Very slowly, very quietly, she turned her head to look out. Whose bed was she under?

Her view was blocked by a lacy white ruffle, but there were little bits of light coming through the lace, so she knew it was still day, though the room was cool as evening. Hmm. Probably no one was in the bed. Probably she could just scoot out and find Molly. She listened with all her might. Nothing but the sound of cicadas outside. Timidly, Miri pushed herself along the polished floor, closer to the lacy ruffle.

"You restless, Mama?"

Miri froze. It was Flo's voice, artificially high and sweet, but definitely Flo's. Two worn brown shoes with trim heels appeared through the lace.

"Your head hurting? I'll get you a cloth." There was a rustle and the sound of water dripping and the shoes moved closer to the bedside. Miri's heart was pounding so loud she thought she could hear it knocking against the polished floor. "Now, Mama, I know you're poorly today, but I reckon you'll forgive me for troubling you when you hear what that ungrateful child's gone and done." There was a pause for a long, mournful sigh. "I'm heartsick, Mama."

Mama! She must be talking to Grandma May. This must be Grandma May's bed that Miri was stuck under. But why was Flo sounding like a preacher? And which "ungrateful child" was she talking about? Molly? Miri's fists curled. Liar.

Flo's thin voice continued, "I hate to say it, Mama, but the apple don't land far from the tree. That Pat Gardner was poison—I always said so. Poor

Maudie! Good thing she's in heaven and didn't live to see the day." There was a silence, and Miri could practically hear Flo shaking her head sadly. Grandma May didn't move. Miri wondered if she could.

Flo took a breath, "Now, you won't believe it, Mama, but I'm telling you the truth: that ungrateful girl ran away!" Miri clamped her lips tight to keep from crying out. *No.* Oh no. She was too late, and Molly was gone. She barely listened as Flo said in a shocked whisper, "She *ran away!* After all we did for her. And she stole some of my money to boot! She's a *thief*, Mama. My own flesh and blood! She stole twenty dollars from my chicken money, just like a common thief. Good thing Horst found her down on the quarry road, or we'd have had to go to the sheriff, and I'd have died of shame!"

Horst found her. Miri winced. Where was Molly now? If only she could get out from under the stupid bed and find her!

Flo sniffed, like she was holding back tears. "I know you'll agree with me, Mama, when I tell you that I cannot have a criminal in my home. If she's lying and thieving now, I hate to think what she'll be up to next. It's for you, Mama. I've got to protect

you, now that you're too poorly to protect yourself."
She gave a little sob. Miri thought she was over-
doing the drama a little. What was her point?

She saw when Flo went on. "I know you won't
blame me when I tell you I've decided that I have to
put her in a home. It's perfectly nice—maybe even
too good—a boarding school for children who need
a firm hand. First thing tomorrow, that's where she
goes." Despite all her efforts to sound sorry, Flo
couldn't keep the excitement from her voice.

Under the bed, Miri writhed with impatience.
Where was Molly now?

Flo's voice, sticky-sweet, went on. "I want you to
look into your heart, Mama. We're all of us trying
to do what's best for Maudie's little girl. But she's not
one of us. She's a Gardner through and through, and
that's the truth. You knew Pat Gardner was no good
before any of us, Mama—you said so, right out, the
first time you met him. And remember how you
cried the day he married Maudie?" Her words
marched out as though she'd memorized them. "If
you leave this land to Molly, you know that Pat
Gardner will swoop down on her like a duck on a
june bug the minute he gets wind that you're gone.

He'll sell the house and the farm right out from under me. Me, your own daughter, and your grandchildren, who love you so. That isn't what you want, is it, Mama? Is it?"

The worn brown shoes were pressed up against the ruffle now, and Miri could hear the greedy sharpness in her voice. "You got to change the will now, Mama. You don't want it all to end up in Pat Gardner's hands, do you? 'Cause that's what'll happen if you leave the property to Molly. She's a Gardner. She's not one of us." Her voice was urgent. "All you got to do is point. Just point one little finger and show me where you put it. I know you can do it, Mama—" She broke off as heavy footsteps entered the room. "What?"

Miri stiffened at the sound of Horst's growl. "She's locked up tight. Got the key right here in my pocket," he said proudly. In spite of him and his key, Miri was flooded with relief. Molly was safe and inside the house. The very worst thing hadn't happened. A band of fear that had been pressing on her heart fell away. But, she reminded herself, that means it's all up to me now. A new band of fear began to circle around her stomach.

"Why's it always cold in here?" Horst muttered. "Steaming hot everwhere else."

"Shhh," whispered his mother. "You know how she is."

"Aw, don't go on about that. Full of baloney. You getting anywhere with her?"

"Can't tell. She don't even move. Not even her eyes."

Horst grunted. "Old biddy's lost her marbles," he mumbled.

"Hush your mouth," snapped Flo.

"All right, all right. But I'm hungry, Ma. Hard work, catching that kid. And she caught it, too." He snorted with pleasure.

I hate you, Horst, thought Miri.

Flo sighed. "All right. I guess I said everything I had to say." She raised her voice into a sweet singsong. "Well, Mama. I hope you heard me. You just rest. I'll be back with your dinner in a bit." Heavy feet and sharp heels moved away. A door closed.

Miri counted to sixty. Then she counted to sixty again. When she poked her head out from under the ruffle, the bright sunlight made her eyes water, but a curlicue of fresh air ruffled through her hair.

The room was very quiet. No place is this quiet in the twenty-first century, thought Miri.

Awkwardly, pulling the CD player behind her, she rose to her feet and turned toward the bed. She didn't know what she expected, but what she saw was not it. A pair of the brightest blue eyes she had ever encountered snapped and sparkled at her. They were not the eyes of a sick old lady. They were bright and laughing—and they knew her. She knows who I am, thought Miri in astonishment. "Hi," she whispered.

The old lady nodded but said nothing.

"I'm here for Molly." Miri had the strangest feeling, light and bubbly. It was almost like the feeling she had when she was pulled through the glasses to another time, minus the sickening feeling. Everything around her shimmered and trembled, except for the old woman on the bed, who seemed, despite her bent shoulders and papery skin, to be as solid as forever. She *was* magic, Miri knew. The room seemed to spin a bit. Secured by those brilliant blue eyes, Miri took a breath, and the room seemed to still. "I'm here for Molly," she repeated in a croak.

Wordlessly, the old woman smiled and pointed to the door. *Go.*

"Okay," said Miri. She wanted Grandma May to reassure her, to tell her that her plan was a good one. "I figured it out, I think," she whispered. "I can't take Molly home right away, can I? We've got to make Horst run away, and then we've got to get one lens in the barn and the other stuck to the wall so I can find them in my time. Right?"

The bright eyes sparkled at her.

"Right. Okay." Miri was half talking to herself now. "He's locked the door to her room, so I'll have to go through the attic. Which means I've got to start in my brothers' room. Right?"

Still Grandma May said nothing.

"Whose room is it in 1935? I know it's not Sissy's." An alarming thought struck her. "It's not Horst's, is it?" She looked at the old lady, who smiled. "Well, even if it is, I'll just deal with it. Right?"

Grandma May pointed to the door.

"Right," Miri answered herself.

Stepping out of the cool bedroom, she paused. The hallway was stifling, and for a moment she stood frozen. Which time am I in? A sudden bellow released her. *"Sis! Dinner!"*

Miri flattened herself against the wall as Sissy swished down the stairs. Chairs scraped against the floor, followed by the rattle of silverware. This was good news—Horst would be busy stuffing himself for a while. Miri slithered around the newel post and up the stairs. Past Sissy's room, and on to her brothers' room. It *was* Horst's—a pair of giant work boots next to the bed told her that—but it wasn't what she thought Horst's room would be like. Horst was a lot neater than her brothers. His dresser was bare except for one comb and one brush, perfectly straight. The bedspread didn't have even a single wrinkle. Miri thought it was kind of eerie.

Also unlike her brothers, Horst had a door on his closet, and it was shut. Cautiously, Miri tiptoed across the silent room and opened the door without a sound. Inside, she saw that the closet was just as clean as the room, with every shirt hanging neatly. Only the ladder looked familiar, reaching up to the attic door. Everything was still; everything was about to happen. Miri felt prickles of panic dancing down her spine. *Hurry.* It wasn't easy to climb a ladder while holding a CD player, but Miri did it in about five seconds. With shaking hands, she shoved open the door to the attic, slung the CD player inside, and hoisted herself after it.

And there was Molly, standing like a statue in the slatted light.

For one single, stunned second, they stared in silence, and then they both started talking at once: "Where'd you *go*?" Molly babbled, her hands skittering wildly through the air in front of her. "I waited and waited—and Horst was in the barn, so it took forever—but then when I finally got out there—"

"I went back by mistake." The words came tumbling out. "I put on my glasses. I had them in my pocket, but I forgot them, and then when I saw Horst—he has this box, and you're right, he's a thief—and—"

They both broke off and smiled at each other.

"Boy, am I glad to see you," said Miri. "I was really worried."

"Tell me everything," said Molly. "Slow, this time."

Miri explained. About Horst and the barn and her broken glasses and seeing him hide stuff and being taken back to her own time and searching for

Molly's glasses and getting her own pair and finding Horst's box and coming back under Grandma May's bed. When she finally stopped talking, she noticed that Molly's gray eyes were filled with tears.

"You're going to take me home with you?"

"Yeah, of course," said Miri. "That's how come it took me so long to come back—I had to get new glasses so we can use them to go home. Mine got totally wrecked when I went back last time, and I didn't think they would work."

Molly said slowly, "I thought you didn't want to run away with me. I thought that's why you left."

"No. I left by mistake," Miri said again. "I didn't know my glasses would take me home. I just put 'em on to see what Horst was up to. And then—boom— I was home."

"And you came back." Molly sounded as if she didn't believe it. "You came back to get me?"

"Yeah."

Molly was silent for a moment. And then she smiled, a dazzling, all-the-lights-on smile. "Oh boy! Isn't that what you always say?"

"Yup."

They grinned at each other.

Then Miri said, "I heard Horst say he caught you running away."

Molly made a face. "Yeah, he caught me. Look." She pulled up the short sleeve of her dress, and Miri saw five fat bruises on her arm.

"I hate that guy," said Miri. "I really, really hate him."

"Me too," said Molly. "I was hiding in the woods, and he found me and drug me back here and locked me in my room. I fought, but he's a lot bigger than I am, and I was scared to get him too mad. I was just fixing to run away again, now they're at dinner. That's why I came in here." She smiled. "But I guess I won't bother."

"I heard your aunt say she was going to take you to some home. She was trying to tell your grandma that you were a thief or something and that your grandma shouldn't leave you anything in her will."

"You heard that?" Molly's eyes blazed. "All they care about is money! Grandma May didn't say anything, did she?"

"No. Nothing. Can she talk?" asked Miri curiously.

After a moment, Molly said, "She ain't talked in a while."

Miri saw the shadows on Molly's face and

changed the subject. "I've got to say, your grandma looks like a fairy," she began. "I didn't really believe you before, but when I saw her, I could see what you meant. She looked at me like she knew me."

"She is a fairy," Molly said firmly. "They pretend they don't believe in it, but they know it's true. Back when she could talk, they were sweet as pie to her, 'cause they were afraid she'd do something to them. You should have seen Horst, acting like Sunday school whenever she was nearby. Almost killed him." She paused. "Wish it had."

Once again, there was the sound of chairs on the floor in the dining room below.

"Let's get out of here," said Miri nervously. "We're right above Horst's room."

Without a word, Molly lifted the flap that led to the secret bench in her closet. She beckoned to Miri, who followed. They tiptoed from the closet into Molly's room.

"My mom is putting up wallpaper just like this right now," whispered Miri, looking at the pink-flowered walls.

"Your mom is?" Molly looked at her shyly. "What's she like?"

"My mom?" Miri paused. It was hard to say what

her mom was like. "She has brown hair and brown eyes. She teaches English at Thomason College. She's—she's—" Miri had never thought about what her mother was like before. "She says funny things. Or maybe she just says regular things in a funny way. She makes French toast for breakfast. She likes old movies." Miri realized as she said it that they wouldn't be old movies to Molly. "You guys will love each other."

"We will?" Molly still looked shy. "Tell me about the rest of them. Do you have brothers and sisters?"

"Didn't I tell you?" Strange—usually it was the first thing anyone knew about her. "We're a one-in-fifty-thousand family because we have two sets of twins. There are my older brothers—Ray and Robbie—they're twelve and totally annoying, but also funny sometimes. And there are my little sisters, Nell and Nora, who are pretty cute but do a lot of bad things like eating ice cream for breakfast and making paste in the bathtub. They're four. And then there's my dad, who goes around lecturing about geothermal energy, which I sort of understand, but not really. He likes math and science and stuff."

"Ray and Robbie. Nell and Nora," repeated Molly. "Molly and Miri."

Hey. Miri had never thought of that.

They heard Sissy's voice in the hallway below. ". . . over to Lottie's, but I can't find my gloves."

"Well, get a move on and I'll drive you over there. I got to get out to Beeton's this afternoon. She says the whole flock are sickening from the heat, but I reckon she ain't . . ." Flo's voice faded as she moved away down the hall.

"Just let me find *my gloves,*" Sissy said irritably.

"Don't know why you gotta wear gloves over to Lottie's. Y'all playing Mrs. Roosevelt?" It was Horst's voice.

"Oh Horst, shut up." Sissy's voice was muffled. "It's a tea party. You got to wear gloves to a tea party."

"Ooh, a *tea party,*" Horst snickered. "Bunch of snot-nose girls. Would you care for a *biscuit*?"

Flo said, "And what're you doing this afternoon, son?"

"Watching the prisoner." Horst slapped his chest in a satisfied way.

"You could go sit with Mama. She might appreciate your company."

"Pah!" Horst snorted. "She don't care who's there. She don't even know."

"And besides," said Sissy sweetly, "Horst's scared of her."

"I ain't! Shut up your mouth!"

"Don't you lay a finger on me! Ma!" Sissy squealed.

"All right, stop it now! Horst, leave your sister alone. You got your gloves, girl? Let's get a move on. I want to get back by five."

"I suppose I'll have to walk home in the dust." Sissy sniffed.

"Cow," said Horst.

"Shut up, Horst." The noise of clattering heels faded as they walked away. There was a silence.

"You hungry in there, runt?" Horst called up the stairs.

Miri froze.

"No!" Molly called back.

"You're lying!"

Molly said nothing.

"Answer me!" he demanded.

Molly said nothing.

"Answer me or I'll come make you!" he shouted.

Miri and Molly heard his heavy feet on the narrow stairs and looked at each other in horror.

"All right—I am hungry," said Molly quickly. "I'm awful hungry."

They could hear his heavy breath outside the door. "Bet you'd like some pie, huh?" he said in a low voice. "Had some of that peach pie for dinner, and it sure was tasty."

Molly's hand reached out to clutch Miri's tightly, and they both stared at the door. Two inches of wood, thought Miri. The only thing standing between us and total disaster. She watched Molly take a little gulp of air and say, "Oh, Horst, can I have a piece?" Her voice was thin and sad. "Just a little piece?"

Miri closed her eyes and silently commanded him to go away. Go to the kitchen, she thought. Go anywhere but here.

"Din't hear you say please," he said softly. They heard his hand on the doorknob.

Please don't come in, prayed Miri.

"Please, Horst," Molly begged pathetically. "Please, will you go get me some pie?"

"*Please, Horst,*" he repeated mockingly. "That's

begging, runt, and you know what they say—
beggars can't be choosers. You don't get no pie, girl,
not after all the trouble you caused. Fact is, I oughta
give you a whaling just for asking. But now you
made me hungry. So I'll tell you what I'm gonna do
instead," he guffawed. "I'm gonna go cut myself a
nice big piece of pie. And then I'm gonna sit myself
down and eat it. It's gonna taste fine. And *then,* if I
ain't too tired after that, I'm going to go out in the
yard and cut me a switch off of one of them apple
trees. And then I'll pay you a little visit. How's that
for a plan, runt?"

Molly's knuckles were white. She tightened her
jaw and said nothing.

"Mm-mm, that pie is gonna taste good!" Horst
crowed. He gave one of his pig snorts and lumbered
down the narrow stairs.

There was a pause, and then both girls let out a
long breath.

Miri saw tears glistening in Molly's eyes, and suddenly her heart was pounding, not with fear but with
rage. Wave after wave of fury flowed over her, until
she was tingling with it. "He's a ratface, pigbag creep,"
she whispered fiercely to Molly. "We'll get him."

Molly shook her head.

"Yes, we will," insisted Miri. "We have to anyway."

Molly brushed roughly at her cheeks. "What do you mean? I thought we were going to your time."

Miri patted the glasses case inside her shirt and thought longingly of home. "Not yet," she said. "There's a couple of things we have to do first." She explained about putting the first lens back on the baseboard in their room and the second back in the barn. Then she told Molly what she had learned from old Mr. Guest, describing Horst's final appearance in the drugstore, shaking and terrified. "I was scared," she confessed. "I was scared that he'd hurt you—or something—and that's why he ran away."

Molly looked confused. "But—wait—if that's the way he tells it, isn't that the way it has to happen?"

"No." Miri leaned forward. "No. That's the thing. We can change what happens. We *are* changing it. But we still want Horst to run away, because if he just hangs around here for the next seventy years, he'll probably take the glasses out of his box in the barn, and then they won't be there for me to find in my time. And if I don't find your glasses, then I can't be here now. See what I mean?" She looked anxiously at Molly.

"Sort of," said Molly slowly. "It makes my head hurt. You want Horst to run away. But not because he"—she took a breath—"kills me."

"Right!" Miri nodded.

Molly gave a little shiver. "Okay. That makes two of us. I don't want him to kill me either. But I don't see how you're going to make him run away. You got a plan?"

"Sure I've got a plan," Miri said. She reached under her shirt and pulled Ray's zombie mask out of her waistband. "My plan is to scare the heck out of him."

Molly looked at the limp mask and her eyes began to glow. "Oh *yes*," she whispered. "Oh yes. I've been waiting for this my whole life."

HORST BAINS LIKED a quiet house. Nothing suited him better than a long afternoon without his mama nagging him about chores or Sissy sashaying about. Yessir, a man's home was his castle when all the loudmouth womenfolk left it. Course, there was the runt, but she was in the jug. And tomorrow, she'd be gone forever! He chuckled to himself, his sides shaking like pudding. Got her out of my hair, he thought, and brushed a microscopic bit of dust off his bedspread. Suddenly he remembered that he had promised her a good switching. The pie had taken it right out of his mind. Should he go out to the orchard and cut himself a branch? Naw—too hot. He'd do it later. It would be something to look forward to.

Horst yawned. He could go look for Gran's will. It was down in her room somewhere, he knew that. He could just go right in and root around for it. She wouldn't be able to say a word. She weren't never going to talk again—anyone could see that. Horst pictured those bright eyes resting on him, and he cracked his neck abruptly. Naw—he was too tired. He'd let Mama do it. She shoulda done it already, but she didn't want to upset the old bat. Mama was surely stupid sometimes. He reached out to straighten the comb and brush on his dresser. There. That was better.

. . .

Upstairs, Miri's hands were sweating. Why had she thought this would work? She had never scared anyone in her life. She stared miserably at Molly, who seemed, on the other hand, to have complete confidence in their success.

"Now," Molly was saying briskly. "What are you going to wear?"

Miri hadn't thought about it. They were doomed. She could practically feel Horst's meaty hands on her neck. She wished she didn't have such a good imagination. "A sheet?" she suggested in a weak voice.

Molly pursed her lips critically. "A sheet seems too babyish. Also not scary enough. We've got to freeze his blood."

Miri's stomach was beginning to hurt a lot.

Molly tugged on one braid, surveying her room. "Ooh, I've got an idea. Flo put her mangy old fur coat in my closet." She started giggling. "We could cut it up, and you'd look like an animal."

"You think he'd fall for it?" Miri said doubtfully.

"Horst? He thinks Flash Gordon is real," said Molly. "He'll fall for it."

"I'm scared," blurted Miri.

"Scared of what?"

"What if he kills us both?" said Miri in a small voice. "What if that's the new ending?"

Molly sat back on her heels, her gray eyes on Miri's. "We have to do it, don't we? Otherwise, he could wreck everything, right?" Miri nodded. "Okay, then. When you have to do something hard, you may as well run toward it."

"So it will be over fast?"

"Yeah, but also because it takes your mind off how scared you are."

She was right, Miri knew. "Okay." Miri swallowed. "Let's see that coat."

Flo's coat hung down to Miri's ankles, and its black fur fell off in clumps when she put it on. Molly gleefully destroyed what was left of it, cutting off the collar and hacking the arms and bottom into long strips. When she was done, it hung in lumpy shreds around Miri's arms and legs. Molly buttoned it up with the buttons inside, so it didn't look like a coat. Miri stared at herself in the mirror on the dresser. Great, she thought. I look like a big, sick dog. Horst might think I have rabies, but he's not going to think I'm a zombie. The whole idea was seeming stupider and stupider. Maybe they should just take the chance and go home. She looked down at Molly, who was busily yanking fur off her sleeves.

Molly glanced up and saw Miri's face. "He'll fall for it," she said firmly.

. . .

Horst heaved himself onto his bed with a groan. He picked up the comic book that lay on his bedside table and inspected the bright cover. Tarzan, with his hand cupped to his mouth, dangled from a vine in front of a herd of elephants. Horst sucked in his stomach. "Ah-ahh-ahh-ah-AH!" he yodeled softly. He let his stomach sag back into pudding. He wished he had a soda pop. Sighing, he opened the comic book and began to read, his lips moving over each word. "Dawlish strained against the ropes that held him, cursing his luck . . ."

. . .

"How do I work it?" Molly asked, frowning at the CD player.

Miri knelt beside her. "See, just press this button, right here—" She pressed, and Deathbag's howls and screams came, very quietly, from the speaker.

Molly was fascinated. "What's that? Why are they screaming like that?"

"It's music. Robbie and Ray think it's supercool." Miri rolled her eyes.

"What do you mean, cool?"

"Cool means—um—good, popular." Molly nodded, but Miri wasn't sure she got it. "You'll understand when you're there. But look, here's the volume. When I get to the bottom of the ladder, turn it all the way up. It's got to be *loud*."

Molly stared at the volume dial. "Cool."

. . .

Outside, the afternoon heat was thick and soft, and inside, Horst's room was dim and quiet. Dim and quiet. The comic book fell forward onto Horst's face. Naptime, he thought sleepily. He spread the comic over his stomach and closed his eyes. Ahh. Nothing like a good nap on a summer afternoon. He cleared his nose in one great, sucking sniff and swallowed noisily.

Ahh.

. . .

"I think we're ready," Molly was saying. "Put on the gloves."

Miri's throat was too dry to reply, but she yanked the gloves over her sweaty hands. She had always hated being in school plays. Even when she had only two lines, she felt like she was going to throw up. And, she reminded herself, nobody killed you at the end of a school play, no matter how crummy you were. Miserably, Miri turned to the mirror and pulled the mask over her head. She regarded the face in the glass. It wouldn't scare a fly. The whole thing was going to be a disaster.

Molly looked up, and her face turned white. "Sweet Jesus!" she whispered.

. . .

Horst drifted into his favorite daydream—the lighted match was almost touching Miss Fletcher's house; she was begging him to pull it away—and he felt himself sinking to sleep.

Ahh.

. . .

"Now!" whispered Molly.

Miri put a trembling hand on the attic door and pulled.

. . .

Creak.

Horst's eyelids snapped open.

Creak.

It was the attic door.

No it ain't, he told himself. Just the runt over there in her room.

Creak.

It was the attic door. Something's coming out,

he thought before he could stop himself. Horst's mouth went a little dry. He'd always hated that attic right up above him. Always. When he was a kid, he'd lie awake, hearing things. Probably just a rat, he thought, trying to ignore the fact that rats can't open doors.

There was a slight pause, and then soft pads told him that whatever-it-was was coming down the ladder.

Horst lay stiffly on his bed, breathing out in little gasps. Maybe he was just imagining it. Sure—that's all it was. It wasn't Gran. Naw. She couldn't. Could she? He didn't believe those stories. *Might be true,* a voice said inside him. *Molly's her favorite. She'd be mad about Molly going to a home.* Bunch of baloney. Horst tried to snort, but it came out thin and squeaky.

The soft pads stopped, and there came a silence that went on for a long time.

See? Ain't nothing there, Horst told himself. Making a gigantic effort, he sat up and looked across the dim room toward the closet door. Ain't nothing there. But the thought came anyway: *Gran's sent something. Gran knows what I done and she's mad.*

The quiet seemed to breathe in and out like an

animal. Horst chewed his lips. Probably, I'm dreaming. Yeah, that's it.

Just the same, he couldn't take his eyes from the closet door. And for some reason he was sweating. He felt a little dribble down his cheek.

The closet doorknob began to turn slowly, and Horst watched. He couldn't blink his eyes. He couldn't move. He was frozen to the bed. A sound came out of him: "Uhh."

All at once, the quiet was shattered by an agonizing scream. Horst almost screamed himself— something was being torn to pieces—something alive! He could hear it! The scream rose and rose, until he thought his head would split in two, and now came a beating, a pounding—grenades! Horst shielded his head with his arms, crying with pain. Now the closet door flew open—Christ Almighty!— it was a monster, a dead man, a half-eaten thing. "Hunh-uhhh," gibbered Horst, shaking his head, trying to clear his eyes. This couldn't be. The dead man wasn't dead, even though his face had been carved in two and his eyeball hung like a gob of white jelly over his cheek. Yellow worms vomited from his mouth, blood glistened wet on his face, and Horst could see the gray brains seeping out of his shat-tered skull, and yet he was *walking*, walking toward Horst. It was an animal, a black animal, it was the devil, it was the living dead, it was *death itself!* It kept walking slowly toward him—putting out its long furry arms—and now the screams were mixed with crashes. It was destroying the house, it was a storm of anger, it was smashing and pounding, it was God, and he was about to be punished for the things he had done.

"Hunhhh!" screamed Horst. He was shaking so hard he couldn't stand, but he rolled up against the head of the bed. "Hunh-a-hunha," he grunted, spit and sweat flying as he trembled.

The dead thing kept coming toward him, its furred flesh hanging in shreds off its corpse, and the screams went on forever—

A narrow black claw jutted out and pointed to-ward his heart. It knew! It knew him! It was going to kill him—it was going to punish him—it was going to *touch him!*

Horst rolled off the bed and fell to the floor. Too terrified to stand, he scrambled for the door on all fours. "Na, na, na, na! Mama! *Mama! Hunh-uh!*" he blubbered, great strings of spit and tears dripping from his face. He looked back once and saw that the dead thing was following him, mouth hungry despite the yellow worms, the white eyeball bobbling against the decayed flesh—it was following him!

The black claw quivered closer, and he cringed away, his legs jerking helplessly against the floor. "Na, na, na . . ."

A thin, dry squeal broke from the beast: *"Get out. Don't come back."* A yellow maggot dropped out of its mouth and landed on Horst's arm.

With a scream, Horst scuttled through the door, slamming it in the dead face. Then he ran for his life.

MIRI SAT DOWN on the floor and shook. Above her, the screams of Deathbag came to a sudden stop, and the silence seemed amazingly loud. Molly scrabbled down the ladder, burst out of the closet, and ran to the window. "Look at him go!" she cried. "He ain't stopping! I wish I could see better. He's kicking up a pile of dust. He ain't moved that fast since Pickett's bull got loose!" She turned to Miri, her eyes shining with laughter. "Tell me how he looked, tell me—" She stopped as Miri pulled the rubber head off. "Are you all right?"

"Whoo," Miri exhaled. "That was scary."

Molly knelt beside her. "How do you mean?"

"I've never done anything like that before," Miri said. She was still shaking. "He was like my nightmares—he was drooling and grunting and sweating. I guess he was really scared. I must have really scared him." It felt weird to do that to someone. It felt weird to be more powerful than Horst.

Molly nodded. "Yeah," she said thoughtfully. "But Horst is a bully. Bullies are always the biggest cowards."

That was true. Miri thought about Horst's low, mean laugh when he said, "And she caught it, too," and she felt her first stab of gladness. "Maybe he'll be better from now on. Maybe I reformed him."

Molly shook her head. "I think you'd have to hit him over the head with a tire iron to reform him. He's been meaner than a rattlesnake ever since he was born."

"I scared him pretty bad," said Miri. She was feeling better and better. They had done it. "He kept saying 'Hunh-ha!'" she giggled.

"Hunh-ha!" said Molly in a deep voice. "Maybe you froze his brain, and he'll only say 'Hunh-ha!' for the rest of his life, like Tarzan. Ain't you hot in that coat?"

Miri looked down at the lumpy black fur. "Boiling. What should we do with it?"

Molly giggled. "Leave it on the bed for Flo to find."

"Wow, she's going to come home, and you're going to be gone and Horst's going to be gone," said Miri as she unbuttoned the coat. "Her whole life is changed."

"Sure is." Molly nodded. "I wonder, though." She paused. "Sometimes I think Flo don't know how to care about anything much, except money. I never saw her cry, not even when her husband died. My uncle Lon." Molly's voice faded away. Then she glanced toward the window. "It's getting late."

Miri sat up, alarmed. "We've got to get going," she said. "We have two more things to do. We have to get one lens out to the barn"—she patted her pocket—"and the other up on your wall. You've still got the first one, right?" she asked anxiously. "The one I came by?"

"I got it," Molly said. "I was keeping it for a souvenir of you. It's on my shelf."

"Go up and get it, okay? I feel like we need to have everything together," said Miri. Molly jumped to her feet and climbed up the attic ladder, returning a moment later with the thin oval of glass in her outstretched palm.

Miri looked at the plain little glass. "I still wonder who put it there the first time."

"If you think about it too long, you're going to go crazy, and then I'll never get to your time," said Molly practically.

"Right," agreed Miri. "Let's go."

"Barn first?"

"Barn first."

. . .

"So long, you dumb old cow," Molly called. She swung the barn door closed, and the two girls padded across the dusty, silent yard for the last time. As they approached the old house, Molly said, "I want to say good-bye to Grandma."

"Okay." Together, they tiptoed up the front stairs and into the hallway. "Why are we tiptoeing?" asked Miri.

"I don't know," said Molly. But they still tiptoed. The whole world seemed hushed and waiting. Even the burning afternoon sun seemed to have stopped in the sky. The birds weren't fussing, and the cicadas held their breath. What were they all waiting for? Miri brushed her hand against the satiny wood that lined the stairs. She would do that again more than seventy years from now. She shivered.

The two girls slipped around the newel post and down the little passage to Grandma May's cool, still room.

The old woman was propped up against a mountain of pillows, her long white hair billowing down around her, her gnarled fingers clasped together. Her eyes sparkled as she caught sight of the two girls, and her thin lips broke into a wide smile. She nodded, and Miri felt the sensation of a light, fresh breeze around her.

"Grandma," began Molly, but her voice cracked and she flew to the bed to wrap her arms around the thin figure. "I have to leave," she whispered.

Grandma May nodded as though she already knew this.

"We—that's Miri, right there—we scared Horst off. You don't have to worry about him anymore. But I'm going to go with Miri, Grandma. She's going to take me home. That's right, isn't it, Grandma?" Molly looked deep into the brilliant blue eyes. "It's magic, isn't it?"

Grandma May nodded.

Without intending to, Miri began speaking. "I don't know what's going to happen when we get home. I'm afraid that my parents won't understand. Or they'll think I'm crazy. Or Molly won't be happy and it will be my fault. . . ." She looked guiltily at Molly. She hadn't meant to say that. What made her start talking?

The old woman lifted her head up from the pillows and looked at Miri with eyes full of love. She wove her fingers among Molly's and smiled. "Magic is just a way of setting things right," she said, in a voice that was as light and lilting as a bird's.

"You can talk?" whispered Molly in astonishment.

Grandma May smiled and turned her brilliant eyes to Miri. "You mustn't be afraid. Either of you."

"Magic is just a way of setting things right," repeated Miri. That sounded hopeful. She didn't really know what it meant, but it made her feel better. She sat down on the edge of the white coverlet.

"Did you know that all this would happen?" asked Molly.

Grandma May shook her head. "There was never only one way it could have happened. You did better than I dared to hope. Both of you."

Miri and Molly exchanged proud glances.

"Did you know who Miri was—before?" Molly was still curious.

May gave her a sly look. "For me, there is no before." She turned her head toward Miri. "Your idea about time being a hallway with different doors is a good one. You were a door that did not appear in the hallway that Molly found herself in. That was an error. Molly's time was supposed to be the same as yours."

"What do you mean, Grandma?" asked Molly, grasping her bony hands.

May sighed. "A slip in time. An error of vision. A mistake that required"—she smiled sideways at Miri—"corrective lenses."

"The glasses," breathed Miri. "You did it!"

"No. *You* did it." May's giggle was like a child's.

Miri suddenly felt lighter than air.

But now the old woman glanced anxiously at the shadows of the trees outside her window. "You haven't finished yet," she said. "You have to replace the first glass."

"We know," Molly assured her. "That's what we're going to do next."

"We'd better do it quick," Miri said nervously.

The whole house lay between them and Molly's room.

Molly nodded, but she made no move to leave the bed. "Grandma." Her voice was full of tears.

"Shh," whispered May, cradling Molly's cheek in her worn hand. "Do you think a little thing like time can separate us? Time means nothing in this house."

Molly looked into her grandmother's eyes. "Will I see you again?"

May smiled. "That depends on your glasses." Her voice was getting weaker. "Go. Go on."

Molly caught up her grandmother's hand and kissed it. "Bye."

Grandma May's eyes were closed, but she smiled.

The two girls rose to leave. As they closed the door behind them, a thin stream of ice-cold air blew through the keyhole.

. . .

They were already starting to sweat as they climbed the stairs. "I'll never see her again," said Molly, her eyes clouded.

Under her bare feet, Miri felt the smooth curves worn in the wood. Time, even seventy or eighty years of it, was nothing to this house. She was beginning to think of the house as a living creature, a being that wanted their happiness. "You never know," she said. "Seems like almost anything can happen in a place like this."

Molly brightened a little. "I reckon you're right about that. It's a funny house." They reached the landing. "Say, I guess we got to go through the attic again, 'cause the key to my room is still in Horst's pocket—"

"Well, if it isn't the jailbird," said a sour voice. "Picked the lock, I suppose?" Sissy stood in the doorway of her room, her irritable mouth pursed. She plucked off her gloves, finger by finger, and slapped them together. "I must say, I'm in no mood to wrestle you back into your room. I thought Horst was watching you."

Molly cleared her throat. "Horst," she began, but no further words came.

Sissy glared at her and pulled a long, deadly looking pin from her straw hat. "Cat got your tongue?" she said coldly. It was only then that she seemed to catch sight of Miri. "And who is this urchin? One of your little friends? Go home, little girl. I'm sure your mother wouldn't want you to associate with *her*," she said, jerking her thumb at Molly, but then Miri's T-shirt and shorts caught her eye. She made a disapproving click with her tongue and said, "On the other hand, maybe you're not much to write home about yourself. Get along. I hear your mother calling you." She waved her hand at Miri.

"No," said Miri.

Sissy looked like she had smelled something nasty. "Pardon *me*, you brat. You clearly were raised in an outhouse. Now get along. I'm too hot and tired to give you a smack, but my brother would be delighted. Horst!"

"Horst won't come," said Miri steadily.

"Miri!" Molly said with a warning look.

"I don't care. I'm not going to let her stop us, not now." Miri looked at Sissy's stiff, plump face, her fussy mouth and prim hair. "Listen, Sissy—"

"Who *are* you?" burst out Sissy. "How do you know my name?"

"I'm from the future," said Miri. Molly's eyes widened, but she said nothing. "And I'm taking Molly home with me. Your mom isn't going to throw her in that orphanage place, and neither of you is ever going to have to deal with her again. But at the moment, we've got things to do, so you can just butt out!" Miri was flushed with anger. She wasn't going to let any snotty teenager boss her arou— A sudden thought made her freeze. Sissy was going to end up with the house. Miri's own family bought it from her. At some point, Sissy was going to put the horrible wallpaper in Molly's room. What if she found the lens and threw it out? The whole thing would never happen! Miri almost groaned out loud. Me and my big mouth!

Sissy turned to Molly. "You have the nicest friends, dear. Get to your room afore I take a belt to you!" For a second, she sounded like her brother. She whirled around to Miri. "And as for you, I'm going to call the sheriff in one minute if you don't get your trashy little two-bit self out of my mother's house!" Her eyes were bulging with rage.

Oh boy, thought Miri. I blew it. Molly sent her an agonized look. What to do? Kiss up. Quick! "Sissy," she began in what she hoped was a friendly voice.

"Don't you Sissy me!"

"Let me explain. I really am from the future. Really!" Miri tried to look trustworthy.

"You're a loony!"

"Okay, I'm a loony. But it's true, and it's also true that Molly's going away with me, so you don't have to fuss about her anymore. You and your mom will inherit everything from Grandma May—" Miri could see that caught Sissy's attention.

"What about Horst?" Sissy asked suspiciously.

"Like I said, Horst is gone." Miri didn't know how Sissy would feel about that—he was her brother after all. Better emphasize the money. "So you'll get everything. Everything. You're going to end up with all of it."

"How do you know?"

"I'm from the future," Miri said patiently. She began to get an idea. It might work. "I fixed it all up for you," she said with a big, toothy smile.

"*Nobody* is from the future," cried Sissy, stamping her foot. "I don't know what you're talking about!"

Molly shot a desperate look at Miri. Should we run for it? her eyes asked.

Miri shook her head slightly. The glass had to stay on the wall. "Listen," she began again. "I'm going to tell you some things that are going to happen. You'll see. I really do know the future." Her brain reeled around, trying to remember things. "America's in a Depression now, right? Well, it'll be over soon."

"When?" asked Sissy.

Shoot! Miri didn't know. When *did* it end? She had to keep talking. "And after the Depression, there's going to be a war, a big one, with Germany. With a guy named Hitler. See if I'm not right."

"Honestly! That's ridiculous. I never heard of him," snapped Sissy.

"Just wait. You will!" Miri could tell she had her attention. "And then we drop a big bomb on Japan, because we're fighting them, too."

Sissy rolled her eyes. Clearly, she didn't believe a word.

Miri thought wildly. "There are going to be people called hippies in the sixties. Lots of colors and—and—music. Rock and roll. There'll be the Beatles. You'll hear about them, for sure. Oh, and some astronauts will go to the moon! I can't remember when, but they do. You'll watch it on television, which is another big thing that's coming. It's like a movie in your own house." She nodded hopefully at Sissy. Believe me, believe me, she thought. "And cell phones! Those are telephones you can carry around in your pocket. And—um—there's Martin Luther King Jr. You're going to hear a lot about him. Just you wait."

Sissy tapped her foot against the floor. "You're nuts."

Miri took the plunge. "And you're going to have children—more than one, I'm pretty sure—and you're going to live here until the twenty-first century, and then your kids are going to take you to live with them in Ohio. Marion, Ohio. You're going to sell the house to the Gill family. You are. And"—Miri took a deep breath—"you're going to put up purple wallpaper with orange vines in Molly's room. Sometime, you're going to do that."

Sissy's floppy mouth hung open. Miri had her now.

"And here's the thing, Sissy. When you do that, when you put up the wallpaper, you're going to find a little piece of glass taped to the wall, right near the floor." Miri's eyes were locked on Sissy's. "If I'm wrong about any of what I've told you, you can take the glass down and throw it away." She heard Molly gulp. "But if I'm right, leave it. Don't touch it and don't let anyone else touch it. Do you promise?"

"What if I don't?" Sissy was trying to look like she didn't care.

"You're going to get all the money, the house. You'll end up with everything. All you have to do is leave the glass alone. Come on, Sissy." Miri struggled to keep her voice calm and quiet.

Sissy didn't say anything.

"If I'm wrong about any of the things I've said, you can do what you want. But if I'm right . . ."

Sissy's eyes moved from Miri to Molly. Molly's gray eyes looked steadily back.

"I'm leaving, Sis," she said, very softly. "I'll never ask you for anything again. Please?"

"Well," said Sissy huffily. "What is it you want?"

"Just promise to leave the glass where it is," pleaded Miri. "That's all you have to do." She waited, almost not daring to breathe.

"Why?"

"Because Molly can't come home with me unless you leave that glass there."

Sissy looked suspiciously from one girl to the other. She tapped her heel. She pursed her mouth. "All right. It's ridiculous."

"You promise?" prompted Molly, straining

forward as if she could push the word from Sissy's mouth.

Sissy sighed deeply. "All right. I promise."

There was a pause. Then—

"Come on!" said Miri, pulling on Molly's hand.

"Yippee!" Molly leaped forward, galloping toward Horst's room.

Sissy whirled around to watch them go, a strange expression on her face. "Molly!" she called.

"What?" Molly paused and looked back.

"Are you really going somewhere?"

"Yes!" Molly shouted.

Sissy fiddled with her gloves for a moment. "I think you're full of baloney and I don't believe a word you're saying, but—well—just in case, sorry," she said quietly. "Sorry about . . . you know."

Maybe she's not so bad, Miri thought, surprised.

Molly grinned and waved. "Don't worry. Bye!"

Leaving Sissy silhouetted against the dark hallway, the girls plunged into Horst's room and swarmed up the ladder. Once in the attic, the slats of light told them that the afternoon was moving into evening, and they hurried, bumping their heads and knees, through Molly's secret passageway for the last time. Out of the closet and kneeling by the base-board, Molly drew the fragile glass from her pocket. "Hope it doesn't break," she whispered. "It's got to last a long time."

"It lasts," Miri assured her.

Molly lifted the tiny glass to her eye and peered through it. "Who knows when I'll get another chance to see clear," she said.

"You can get another pair when we get home," said Miri confidently. "Mom isn't just going to kick you out. She'll get you some glasses, I bet you any-thing."

"Why should she?" said Molly doubtfully. "She doesn't know me from Adam." She reached out a finger to stroke the lens and sighed. "Oh well. I'm getting pretty used to everything blurry."

Molly peeled a piece of cellophane tape from a roll—Miri supposed that dispensers hadn't been in-vented yet—and they attached the delicate glass to the baseboard. It glinted there like a little window.

"There it is," said Miri. "Just where I found it." It would wait patiently for her, right there, for many years. She turned to Molly. "You ready?"

Molly grinned. "Yup."

Miri pulled out the second case, the one containing her new glasses. "I think it'll be safer if we both look through a lens," she said, cracking the plastic frame and trying not to imagine what her mother was going to say about that. She held out half a pair of glasses to Molly.

"Let's hold hands. Don't you think?" asked Molly anxiously.

"Good idea." Miri took Molly's thin brown hand in hers. "Okay, on the count of three, lift it up and look through it with one eye. Gotta keep the other one closed. Okay?"

"Yes." Molly's voice was tense.

"One." Molly's hand clenched hers. "Two." Miri was having trouble catching her breath. *"Three."*

THEY STRETCHED UP against the gum of time while Molly's room sank down, and then, with a sickening heave, the two girls were pushed through, gasping, into the center of the ten-walled room. For the first moment, they just hung on to their stomachs.

Miri blinked.

The afternoon was only long shadows now, and pink light. But—

"Is this my room?" breathed Molly, staring.

"Yes, but it didn't look like this when I left," Miri replied, turning about to survey the wreckage. Purple wallpaper hung in long strips from the walls, showing jagged triangles of yellow plaster in between. All of the furniture had been pushed to the center of the room and covered with an assortment of plastic sheets. But none of this was what made Miri suddenly breathless.

"What?" said Molly. "Bet you're glad you're getting new wallpaper. That's the ugliest stuff I ever saw in my whole life." She plucked a piece from the wall and brought it close to her face. "Plug ugly. Sissy got it cheap, I can tell."

"Molly?"

Molly spun slowly around, trailing wallpaper from her fingers. "We did it, didn't we? I wasn't so sure—but here I am! In my room, or your room, or our room"—she spun faster—"my room, your room, our room!" She laughed. "It's magic! For us!" The wallpaper fluttered behind her.

"Ooh, are you in the doghouse!" It was Robbie and Ray, standing in the doorway.

Molly collapsed dizzily to the floor and stared in silence at the two boys.

"What?" said Miri nervously.

"You are *totally* in the doghouse with Mom," sang Ray. "She had to take down all this wallpaper, and you were supposed to help. Can you say *ball-is-tic*, boys and girls?"

"*We* helped," said Robbie, grinning. "Mom loves our butts."

Miri looked helplessly at Molly, who looked back at her, equally surprised. Why wasn't anyone saying anything about the fact that there was an unknown girl sitting in the middle of the floor? Was Molly invisible?

"I think we're going be seeing some significant upward momentum in this season's stats, don't you?" said Ray in a sports announcer voice. He turned to Robbie.

"Yeah." Robbie grinned. "Despite a weak early season, the boys will be outplaying the girls this summer," he added, holding a nonexistent microphone to his mouth.

"The girls have suffered serious setbacks, due to—"

"Them being girls," Robbie interrupted, laughing.

It was all so normal. They showed none of the hesitation or even politeness they would have in the presence of a stranger. They were exactly themselves. Miri opened her mouth and closed it again. The boys stopped, waiting for her insult. When none came, they turned toward Molly. Did they expect her to say something? Did they even see her? She stared back at them, paralyzed.

Ray shrugged. "Whatever. Let's Wiffle, dude."

"No. Wiffle sucks."

"No, you suck. I'll let you hit first even though it's my turn." Squabbling, the boys descended the stairs and argued their way down the hall and out of earshot. It was completely and totally normal.

"Robbie and Ray?" whispered Molly, after a minute.

Miri nodded.

"Did they see me?"

"I don't know," Miri replied. Something very strange was going on here. She looked over to the cluster of furniture in the middle of the room. "A bunk bed," she said quietly.

Molly followed her glance. "Yeah."

"I don't have a bunk bed," said Miri. Molly's eyes met hers, and they stared at each other in silence. It could only mean one thing, but that one thing was—impossible?

"Try the closet," croaked Molly, making no move to rise from the floor.

"Right." Sidling around the wallpaper and plastic

sheets, Miri peered into the closet. Her collection of pants, coats, party dresses, and jackets was there—but next to it was another set. There were five dresses, a long bathrobe, some jeans, a pink corduroy jacket, and two coats that Miri had never seen before. Slowly, as if moving through water, she dropped her eyes to the floor. Neatly lined up were a pair of shiny black shoes and rubber boots. Tossed casually on top of them were two red sandals and a single sneaker.

Molly joined her in the doorway.

Miri shook her head. "I've never seen some of this stuff before."

"Do you—could it—" The words couldn't find their way out of Molly's mouth.

"It can do anything," breathed Miri.

Before they could say another word, Miri heard her mother's brisk footsteps in the hallway. "Miri? Molly? Are you two up there?"

Molly looked at Miri, and her face was a wild flame of hope.

"We're here," said Miri, her heart thudding.

"And about time, too. I trust that you're peeling the paper off the walls." She was climbing the stairs now.

"Yeah," Miri said hoarsely. "That's what we're doing."

Molly flew to the farthest wall and jerked off a long strip of paper. Her back was toward the door, but Miri saw her hands shaking.

"All I can say is that you two are very lucky that your kind brothers offered to help me today, because if I had had to do this all by myself, I would be a lot madder than I am right now." Mom stood in the doorway, surveying the walls with pride. "I think we did pretty well. If we finish the big pieces tomorrow, we can steam the rest of it off next week when Daddy comes. Then we'll put up your dainty pink roses." She chuckled. "Pink roses. Who would have guessed?" She wandered over to the wall where Molly was tearing paper furiously. "Look at you, working so hard." Casually, she smoothed Molly's hair and then dropped a kiss on the top of her head. Miri could hear Molly gasp. "Well, sweetie, don't wear yourself to a nubbin." She stopped on her way out of the room and nudged Miri gently. "Why don't you help your sister instead of just standing there like a frozen pork chop?" She kissed Miri lightly on the cheek. "Get busy," she growled.

"Okay," said Miri. "Sure. I'll help my sister." Like a sleepwalker, she approached a wall.

"Mama!" yodeled Nell from down the hall. "Nora stapled my socks!"

"Oh Lord," sighed Mom, making for the door. "Dinner in about a half an hour," she called over her shoulder. "And Molly, I forgot to get ketchup. Do you want sour cream on your potato?"

"Sure. Sour cream," rasped Molly.

Mom's footsteps moved briskly away.

Their hands dropped to their sides and they stared at each other.

"Sisters," Miri said.

"Sisters," Molly repeated, her voice solemn. Then an uncontrollable smile blazed across her face. "Is that okay with you?"

"With me?" said Miri incredulously. "Okay with me? It's the best thing that ever happened to me in my whole life!"

"It's impossible, you know," began Molly. "It's totally impossible that I'm just suddenly part of your family. It's completely—*impossible.*"

Impossible! Miri laughed. Nothing was impossible now. "Don't you remember?" she asked. "Magic is just a way of setting things right."

"Everything's right now," said Molly, looking around at the dusty room as though it were a palace.

Miri joyfully ripped a strip of the old paper off the wall. "Just wait," she said. "It's going to get righter and righter."

ANNIE BARROWS always hoped that she would travel to the past and that she would get an attic bedroom, but she didn't have luck with either wish, so she decided to write about them instead. Annie is the *New York Times* bestselling author of *The Guernsey Literary and Potato Peel Pie Society* as well as the popular Ivy and Bean series. Annie lives in northern California with her husband and two daughters.

www.anniebarrows.com

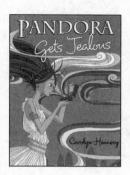  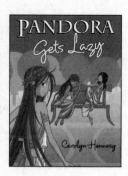